VERY TWISTED THINGS

BRIARWOOD ACADEMY

WALL STREET JOURNAL BESTSELLING AUTHOR

ILSA MADDEN-MILLS

Very Twisted Things
Book Three
Briarwood Academy Series
Copyright © 2015 by Ilsa Madden-Mills

Cover Design by Okay Creations
Editing by Rachel Skinner of Romance Refined
Formatting by Champagne Book Design

Little Dove Publishing
ISBN: 9781094736891

First Edition March 2015
P Second Edition June 2016

For my husband, the best beta reader a girl could have.
You're my Viking, for reals, babe. I love you.

PROLOGUE

"Fairy dust is not real. This I know."
—from the journal of Violet St. Lyons

BOOM!

I, Violet St. Lyons, who once believed herself the luckiest girl in the world, was born on the same day that the Violette–Sells comet was discovered. My parents, two avid stargazers, said it was a sign of how special I was and promptly named me Violet. They claimed my life had been blessed with fairy dust.

At the very least, comet residue.

I'd foolishly believed it for eighteen years, until the moment of my death.

Which was now.

Boom! Another explosion rocked the plane and metal ripped away as a section of the aircraft to my right vanished. Luggage flew through the air. People disappeared. The mom with the baby who'd sat in the aisle across from us—gone. The redheaded flight attendant who'd been collecting trash—gone. Disembodied screams echoed from the surrounding passengers as my own scream took up most of the space in my head. Air sucked at us viciously from the outside as a tornado of people banged around the space and one by one got pulled out into the swirling abyss.

I watched, helplessly transfixed, as I sat between my

parents, gripping each of their hands as the plane we'd boarded six hours earlier for Dublin spiraled toward the Atlantic Ocean. I was going to die. My mother was already dead, a twisted piece of shrapnel sticking grotesquely from her chest as her head lolled around her neck. Blood had already soaked her shirt, yet I refused to let go of her hand. She'd be okay. We were always okay. We were the St. Lyons family of Manhattan, an icon of old money wealth with deep political ties. Page six of the *New York Times* featured pictures of us on a monthly basis. We couldn't die on a plane.

Reality dawned as we plummeted. The yellow breathing apparatus dropped and dangled in my face, taunting me with its pointlessness. Fire and black smoke boiled in front of us where the cockpit had been, and my mind recognized that the pilots had to be dead. Just a few minutes ago, they'd come over the intercom and announced that the plane was making its descent into Dublin Airport exactly on schedule.

Then the first explosion had gone off.

Bits of debris flew around, narrowly missing me. My elderly father grabbed my hand and squeezed, his face drawn back in a horrible grimace. Fear and then horror flickered across his face as he saw Mother, but there was no time to comfort him.

Paralyzed in my seat, we spun like a drunken top, and a part of my brain noticed the sun was rising, its pink tinge lending a soft glow, catching the reflection of clouds and making them silver-lined. The rocky coast of Ireland glittered in the distance. Mocking me. We'd been headed there to celebrate my eighteenth birthday.

Just then my violin case flew past my head from the overhead compartment and crashed against the wall of the plane. Shards flew. I shuddered and wanted to vomit. God, help us. We were here because of me. Our deaths were my fault. I spared a glance at the diamond promise ring Geoff had given me before we'd left. Would the Mayor of New York's son go on without me?

The air was turbulent yet thin, and my chest tightened as dizziness pulled at me. I resisted. Had to stay awake. Had to be with my dad. I was younger, stronger, faster. My eyes went to the gaping hole in the plane. Had to think ahead. Plan. Water would fill up the plane on impact, ensuring we'd sink rapidly.

My fear escalated as the ocean rushed at us, its surface choppy and ominous. I took in a giant breath and braced myself. We hit at an angle, the plane a torpedo as it sliced into the sea. Daddy disappeared, ejected by the impact, and I yanked on my seat belt, unclicking it to go after him. Heart thundering, I sent a final look at my mother. I wanted to take her with me, but she was gone.

Water everywhere, bubbling and gurgling as it filled up the plane. Salt water stung my eyes. People floated by, some alive as they floundered for the opening. I kept my gaze off the dead ones. *Focus. Get out. Only seconds left.*

I swam from my seat and fought my way out of the large hole in the plane, lungs exploding. Burning. I'd been under too long.

Daddy! I caught a glimpse of his red shirt above me and kicked harder.

Up, up, up. Must get up. My arms moved. My legs kicked. Excruciating pain. Ignore it. Almost there. So close that I could see the daylight breaking through the water.

The hottest fire I've ever known lit in my chest. Scorching.

Air. Just want to breathe. Just get to the top. *Please.*

My body rebelled and I inhaled and swallowed water, the

burn racing down my throat making it spasm as I tried to cough it out. I struggled but took in more and more, the cold liquid filling my lungs.

Dark spots filled my eyes. This was drowning.

Exhausted.

Done.

My body twitched. I grew disoriented.

I let go of the fight. My hands floated in front of me.

Oblivion.

Darkness.

No bright lights, no tunnel.

No heaven, no mother, no father.

No comets.

No fairy dust.

CHAPTER 1

"She was music with skin."—Sebastian Tate

Two years later

WHERE WAS SHE?
I stood at the edge of the patio and adjusted my binoculars, spying on the twenty-something girl who lived in the Spanish-style mansion behind us in the Hollywood Hills. And by mansion, I mean a house three times the size of ours with a red slate roof and a huge archaic-looking door on the front. Impressive. The Maserati out front was sick too. Chick was rich, living the dream.

She was also excruciatingly beautiful with her long dark hair and badass violin.

But *who* was she? A Hollywood celebrity like me? Somehow, I didn't think so—mostly because she was always alone.

Last night from my hilltop view, I'd watched her eat a solitary dinner out on her patio, taking in how she sliced into her chicken and then chewed, her head bobbing to the music on her stereo. She'd added a serving of cheese puffs to her plate without a flicker of remorse, and for dessert she'd eaten an entire sleeve of Oreos. Her evening drink was a sniffer of tequila. I didn't judge. Living on the road for five years, I'd had my own share of strange meals.

She was odd.

Since we'd moved in a few weeks ago, I'd concocted all kinds of theories about her. She was a porn star who'd retired and chosen to live out her life in solitude; she was a musician holed up in a mansion, composing an opus that would hypnotize the entire world; or my favorite, she'd killed her last boyfriend with an axe over his refusal to share his cheese puffs and she was now using the house next door as her hideout. Crazy to dwell on someone I didn't know, but there was something about her loneliness that struck a nerve.

My bandmate Spider thought I was just bored. Maybe.

I tapped my foot.

What was taking her so long?

"Is she naked? Otherwise, what's the bloody point in spying on her?" Spider asked me in a stage whisper, coming up behind me in the darkness on the patio. The Englishman sipped on his Jack and Coke.

"She's not out yet," I said. "And, it's not really spying. I just like her music."

He snorted. "Uh-huh. She's fucking hot, isn't she?"

Hot as hell—but I wasn't sharing. I was surprisingly territorial when it came to Violin Girl.

"I think some clubbing would cure you real fast, mate." He did a pirouette dance move that was straight out of our latest music video.

"Dude. Not tonight." I needed a break. The paparazzi were all over me now that I was "fake dating" Hollywood starlet Blair Storm to garner good press.

He threw his hands up to the sky. "You're *Sebastian Tate*, the lead singer of the Vital Rejects whose YouTube video just clocked in at two hundred million views. We're famous, and all you want to do is wait for her to come out." He shook his head.

"It's right odd how you fancy her."

I laughed at his theatrics. I suspected he was drunk. "Coming from the guy with a blue pompadour," I said.

"Don't be jealous." He smoothed his newly dyed hair delicately. "Seriously, I liked you better when you got obsessed with *The Vampire Diaries*."

I snorted. "Ha. Shut the fuck up. *You* love that show."

He grinned. "Never. I hate blood suckers. Fucking pussies."

"Uh-huh."

"I watch macho shows, like wrestling and NASCAR," he insisted.

"Bullshit. You DVR everything on The CW." I snickered.

He lit a cig and sent me a thoughtful look. "You know, I haven't had a shag in a while. You think Violin Girl would like me?"

I inhaled sharply. "She's really not your type. I suggest you stick with your groupies."

"If she's female, she's my type." He waggled his eyes at me.

An image of her playing for him came to mind, and possessiveness zipped up my spine. I slammed my beer down on the patio table. "Keep in mind, we don't know *who* she is or if she's got a boyfriend. She could be married, and we don't need another scandal."

His lips quirked, and I suspected he'd played me all along.

I narrowed my eyes at him. I loved the blue-haired freak, but he could be a pain in the ass.

He popped me on the arm. "Wake up and smell the sexual tension, mate. You dig her, which is the most interest you've shown in a girl in *five* years. I can't help but be fascinated."

I shrugged. Whatever.

"Just go meet her. Knock on her door, pretend you're lost, chat her up. Hell, take Monster with you. Girls love dogs, especially cute white Chihuahuas with ADHD."

"*You're* giving me dating advice?"

He paused and then grimaced. "Scary, huh?"

Spider was a notorious womanizer and generally treated girls like shit.

I sighed. "I don't want to screw up the Blair thing."

Spider got quiet, disapproval radiating off of him. "Blair's a piranha. You must really want this zombie movie."

I nodded. "It's directed by Dan Hing. Apparently, he had a bad experience on his set with a rock star-turned-actor and despises them. But, if I'm dating America's Sweetheart, then I look like Mr. Nice Guy." I paused. "Your arrest last year in Vegas didn't help our image," I said, reminding him of the heckler whose nose he'd busted. "We've had a shit-ton of bad press and I'm trying to fix it."

He jutted out his chin, and I let out a sigh and rubbed my temple. Acting like his dad was wearing thin.

He changed gears. "Emma sent me an email asking if we're going to the Briarwood Academy reunion in September. Are we in or what?"

"She's in charge?" I bit out.

He nodded.

Great. Old feelings of betrayal swept over me as I remembered the fool I'd been for her in high school. She'd used me to make her asshole ex jealous, but the kicker had been she'd gotten pregnant—*and hadn't known who the father was.* Those had been the worst six months of my life waiting for the DNA test to come back. *Me* a father at eighteen? It had seemed like the end of the world.

I made the Catholic cross sign with my hands.

"Aren't you a non-practicing Presbyterian?" He smirked.

"Emma," I muttered. "Just thanking the heavens I escaped being her baby daddy."

"Yeah, glad that award went to Matt Dawson. Total wanker. I bet they're miserable together." He shot me a concerned look. "You *are* going, right?"

My mouth tightened. "I don't want to see Emma." *What if I still had feelings for her?* But I did want to see my older brother Leo and his wife Nora, who'd been one of my best friends at the prep school in Highland Park, Texas.

He stewed on that. "I say we go, get hammered, wreck the school gym—maybe jump on stage and play a song—call it a regular day. I promise to not get arrested this time. Scout's honor."

Movement came from next door, and I put the lenses back on my face. "Shhh, she's out," I said as she walked outside to her patio, carrying her violin. She flicked on her porch lights, and a low whistle came out of me at the sexy red-as-sin robe she wore, its silky material flashing around her long legs as she moved about. Her hair was down, too.

This was new. Where were the usual yoga pants? The ponytail?

She looked like she *knew* someone watched, but that was impossible since our outside lights were off. Even the light from the moon hit our house at such an angle that she shouldn't be able to see us just by glancing over. She'd need a high-powered lens to know I was here.

Spider mumbled something and went back inside, probably to watch The CW—or go clubbing. I barely noticed.

Usually she played facing her rose garden, but this time she walked to the right side of her patio, which faced *us*. Weird. But she didn't play. She just stood there without moving. Staring toward our house. Uneasiness went over me.

What was she doing?

Could she see me?

As if it were a fragile bird, she positioned the violin under her chin and began playing, arms bent and wrist poised, making the most exquisite sounds. And I don't mean classical like Beethoven or Mozart; I mean body-thrashing, blood-thumping, hard-as-hell music that had me rooted to the ground, like she'd slapped iron chains on me.

Dark and seductive notes rose up in the air, and I got jacked up, recognizing a Led Zeppelin song, only she'd ripped its guts out and twisted it into something electric. She pushed the bow hard, upping the tempo abruptly, her movements controlled yet wild. My pulse kicked up and my eyes lingered, taking in the slightly parted toned legs and the way her breasts bounced as she jerked her arms to manipulate the strings.

Her body arched forward in a curve, seeming as if she might break into a million pieces before she finished the piece or climaxed first. Then, her robe slipped off her right shoulder, exposing part of her breast. Creamy and full, it quivered, vibrating as she moved her arms. Her rosy nipple teased me, slipping in and out of the folds of the material, erect from the cool mountain air and deliciously bitable. I pictured my mouth there, sucking, my fingers plucking, strumming her like my guitar until she begged me to—

Stop, I told myself just as an appreciative groan came out. Whoever Violin Girl was, she didn't deserve me lusting after her while she was pouring her heart out with music.

I zoomed in as far as the binoculars would go, watching her surrender to the music as she bent and swayed from side to side with her eyes closed, black lashes like fans on her cheeks. Every molecule in my body focused on her, hanging on to each note she pulled from her instrument.

She finished and kept her head bowed for the longest time, perhaps letting the emotion wash over her like it had me. Then, she bowed to the banana trees and gnomes in her garden, waving her hands in a flourish as she rose.

The entire event was surreal, yet poignant as fucking poetry.

I let out a deep breath I didn't even realize I'd been holding.

Who the hell plays *Stairway to Heaven* with a violin? She did.

Violin Girl was music with skin. She was real and dark and twisted and I wanted to eat her up. I wanted to consume her and every single note she ripped from her violin.

Bam! She snapped her head up, her eyes lasering in on mine, making every hair on my body stand at attention.

And then . . .

Standing there in the moonlight, she untied her robe and spread apart the sides ever so slightly, her movements seeming almost hesitant, as if she'd had to work herself up. Unfamiliar jealousy hit me and I panned out and checked the rest of the patio, expecting to see a lover. Whoever it was, I wanted to rip him apart piece by piece.

And didn't that thought surprise me.

My gaze searched her patio, the backyard, her upstairs balcony. Nothing. No one.

She flicked her dark hair back and stroked the lapels of the robe, her fingers lingering over the lacy material. Suddenly the evening smacked of something *more* than just music. Her arms moved back and forth across the front, opening the robe halfway and then closing it as if she couldn't make up her mind.

My eyes went up, trying to read her face. Still as a statue, the only movement was her mouth as it trembled, her full upper lip resting against the pouty lower one. Tears ran down her face, but they seemed more of a defiant act, her jaw tightly set, her shoulders hunched inward as if she'd held it in too long and was giving in, but not without a fight.

Violin Girl was trapped in a cage of darkness.

It still didn't stop me from holding my breath, silently begging her to bare herself to me. She'd already laid bare her music. Part of me needed the rest of her.

She jerked the robe closed, making me groan in disappointment.

And then she did something completely crazy.

The lonely girl next door flipped me the bird.

CHAPTER 2

"Sixteen minutes. That's how long it took for the emergency
helicopters to reach the crash site where Flight 215's right wing had
been bombed by terrorists. Reports said they found me floating on top
of a seat cushion, my legs dangling in the water, although I have no
memory of getting there. Covered in cuts and bruises, I had a broken
leg and wasn't breathing when they pulled me up in a harness. The
truth was, the real Violet died that day in the Atlantic."
—from the journal of Violet St. Lyons

CHEST HEAVING, I RAN BACK IN THE HOUSE FROM THE PATIO AND
came to a stop in front of the fireplace, the enormity of my
performance settling on my shoulders. I panted. I clutched
my pounding heart. Mortified. Excited. Good lord, I'd played for
Blond Guy.

I'd nearly stripped for him.

I wholeheartedly blamed the tequila I'd consumed earlier.

My hands went to tapping against my leg erratically, my
new go-to reflex since the crash. Without fail, if I were stressed,
my hands bounced around, trying to ground me.

I groaned and paced around the den like a madwoman.

No way to deny it—I was officially an exhibitionist.

Blond Guy had moved in a few weeks ago on a bright and
sunny morning in May without a cloud in the sky. I'd been out
on the back patio, messing around with some of the plants,
when he'd raced down the road in his gray Hummer and pulled

in at the house behind mine. A girl with crazy red hair and a man bigger than the Blond Guy had pulled in behind him in a black Escalade. Siblings? Most definitely family, I'd decided as they carried suitcases and bags in the house, the sounds of their laughter echoing across the grass that separated our secluded properties. Like a shadow, I'd hidden behind a palm tree and squinted across the distance to watch them. I felt silly and tried to tear my eyes away, but when Blond Guy pulled out a guitar—and not just a regular guitar, but a Gibson Les Paul, the same model as my dad's—I'd been lost.

A musician.

My interest had quickened.

Yesterday, thanks to my handy telescope, I'd been shocked when I'd caught him watching my house with binoculars right at the time when I usually played my violin outdoors. Immediate anger filled me—along with a good dose of something I couldn't identify. Anticipation? Fear? Most definitely both.

Words like *creep* and *Peeping Tom* brushed at my mind, but somehow I refused to associate him with those. The truth was, I hadn't knowingly played for anyone since the crash because the thought of having eyes on me gave me the shakes and made me want to hurl. My therapist called my fear PTSD (Post Traumatic Stress Disorder); I called it cowardice. I hated it.

I used to be Violet St. Lyons, violin prodigy, but now I was just a freak.

Either way, my music career was ruined. They don't let pukers play in the New York Symphony; it kinda ruins the show.

But *he* was watching me, obviously listening to my music.

And I'd wondered if I could play knowing he was out there.

My therapist said I should bite the bullet and play on stage whether I lost my cookies or not. Her theory sounded simple, but doing it was another thing. *The remedy is in the poison* my father had liked to say, and that was the one voice in my head I gravitated toward.

I wanted to try. I *wanted* to push myself.

Like the flakes in a snow globe, music has danced around in my head since I was a little girl, and without it, I was lost.

I'd already lost my parents.

I tightened the belt on my robe and let out a puff of air. That's why tonight—after those shots—I'd found some backbone, slipped on my robe and gone out to perform. Technically, I hadn't been able to see him, so I hadn't known for sure if he watched, yet I'd felt his eyes on me. Burning. Waiting for me to take it all off.

Which begged the question, did he watch because he liked my sound or did he watch because he was attracted to me? Probably the first. I wasn't much to look at lately, not with my yoga pants and T-shirts.

Nerves settled by my breathing exercises, I headed to the kitchen where I scrounged for a celebratory chocolate bar and a soda. My brain knew my eating habits were out of control since my parents were gone, but I couldn't seem to muster up the effort to do better. I devoured the Hershey bar and then headed to bed, checking my phone on the way. I sighed. No one had called. My friends from rich kid prep school hadn't. My fellow musician friends from the Manhattan School of Music hadn't. Even my promise-ring-kinda-fiancé Geoff who was now dating a fancy socialite hadn't. They'd given up on me. Not that I blame them, of course; I'd pushed them away. And really, who'd wait two years for me to get my shit together when it might not ever happen? I swallowed down a sip of soda and burped. At least alone I didn't have to worry about the niceties.

I eventually crawled in bed, but by two in the morning, sleep still eluded me, and I considered taking one of the sleeping pills my doctor had prescribed. Instead, I got up and went out to the balcony to peek through my telescope. It was dark at his house and hard to make out details, but I found him sitting out on his patio, a guitar between his legs and a beer on the table. I zoomed in my Celestron 2000, my eyes taking in the tattoos that snaked up his muscled biceps that my fingers suddenly itched to touch. I bit my lip. He was beautiful. Transfixed, I watched him smile to himself as he'd play a few strings then stop and jot down something on a piece of paper. Writing music?

Who was he?

Who was I?

Two years ago, I'd been a girl surrounded by fairy dust. I still vividly remembered walking into our Upper East Side apartment, not a clue that my parents had planned a surprise trip to Ireland for my birthday and we'd be leaving for the airport within the hour. They'd made such a big deal of it, trying to get me to guess what my present was. This had included my dad doing his crazy version of the river dance while my mom pulled out a stuffed leprechaun and danced along. They'd been so silly. Fun. Everyone had loved my parents, even the crabby old lady in 4A who hated everyone.

But thinking of my past perfect life was a knife in my heart, so I pushed it away. Instead, I studied Blond Guy's chiseled face and my imagination went wild as I imagined me showing up at his house, wearing nothing but my robe and carrying my violin. He'd open the door without a word and let me inside. I'd play for him while his hands touched my skin.

Bringing me back to life.

At that, I shivered as warmth infused my skin, pooling in my lower body. I got back in bed and relaxed—effortlessly—for the first time in months and drifted off to sleep. Yet, instead of my usual nightmares about the crash, I dreamed of him. I dreamed he sat by my bed and watched me sleep, that he reached out his hand and pushed hair from my face. His touch made me tingle all over, and even in my dream, my consciousness recognized that I wanted to play again for the boy next door.

&

The next morning, I walked into Java and Me, the local coffee joint and independent bookstore where I came each morning after my run. Decorated in black and white, it was heavy on modern style and Hollywood celebrities. It was also close to my neighborhood and the local market where I did my shopping.

Coming here was my routine. Next, I'd do a slow drive-by at the orphanage on Campbell Street, the one with the lake out front with the ducks. I'd never been inside, but maybe today I'd pull into the parking lot and go inside and meet Mrs. Smythe, the director. She'd called me several times this past month to help plan a benefit gala, and I knew I couldn't put off meeting her forever. That orphanage was mine. Part of the reason I moved here.

I got my latte and found a seat next to the window.

Blair Storm and her usual entourage took the large table next to me. With big boobs and puffy lips, she was a thirty-something starlet who'd been plucked, highlighted, and mani-pedied to perfection. Pamela Anderson from Baywatch came to mind. She tended to spend most of her time primping and checking the waddle under her neck.

I sighed. I sounded jealous. I guess she *was* extremely pretty if you liked white-blond hair and flashy clothes. I paled in comparison. Literally. I needed to work on my tan. I resolved to get a bathing suit and lay out by the pool. Maybe Blond Guy would want to come over and join me? No. That was crazy. I didn't need to get involved with anyone.

A delicate hand tapped on my shoulder, interrupting my thoughts, and I turned to meet a pair of the thickest, longest set of fake eyelashes I'd ever seen. A spider could live there and no one would ever know.

"Excuse me, I'd like a refill," Blair said sweetly, thrusting her recycled paper cup with the Java and Me logo in my face.

I blinked. *Really?* She'd seen me here a dozen times as a customer.

"Sorry. I don't work here." I indicated my e-reader and latte. "If you want more coffee, the employees wear black and white— you know, the people with aprons and name badges." I smiled. I'd grown up with girls like her, Park Avenue Princess types who thought everyone owed them.

"Your shirt *is* black and white." She nudged one of her girl-friends, and they both burst out in a fit of laughter.

I looked down at my black Ramones shirt and grimaced. Band shirts and flip-flops hadn't always been my everyday attire. At one time, slinky and soft had been my go-to fabric. Couture even. I put my back to Blair, hoping she'd forget about me and move on. Although it was unlikely, the thought of her realizing *who* I was gave me hives. Literally. An itch had taken up on my back, between my shoulder blades.

She jabbed me on the arm again, this time more insistent.

I tensed and pulled as far from her as I could.

"Honey," she said, the syllables drawn out and sugary enough to make me gag. "Don't you know who I am? I'm Blair Storm. I just wrapped up a James Cameron movie and a Maroon

5 music video with Adam Levine." She preened as one of the girls in her group clapped excitedly. I halfway expected her to take a bow. "I'm one of the biggest stars in Hollywood, and if you don't know that, then you must live under a rock. Now, be a sweetie and get me a refill."

In my head, I tapped out "Rip Her to Shreds" by Blondie on my violin.

I scowled. "I'm fully aware of your awesome magnificence. And I'm not your *sweetie*."

"What did you say?" she said, straightening up in her seat, glossy lips now in a straight line. The occupants around us froze, eyes bouncing from me to her. Even the manager speared me with a glare saying, *Don't bother the talent!*

Anger bubbled up, and I opened my mouth to let her have it like I would have before the crash, but I froze, blood rushing to my face. My free hand—the one that wasn't clutching the table—twitched to tap.

She thrust her cup at me again, eyes glittering like hard diamonds. "I must have misheard you."

I ignored her and turned my head away, tucking myself close to the window. Pretty soon, I'd be splattered against it like a bug.

"Hello? Are you deaf?" she snapped, and I knocked my coffee over as I jerked up from my seat. Brown liquid seeped across the table and dripped on the floor. I watched it spread, unable to get napkins, unable to move. Paralyzed. My gut knew a panic attack was not far behind. I took up panting and tapped my leg.

She eyed me, her gaze flicking over my hands. "Clean-up on Aisle Stupid," she called out over a mock microphone as the rest of her group tittered.

Every eye in the place swiveled to stare and I had a flashback to the day I'd gotten out of the hospital in Dublin. Reporters, photographers, gawkers—they'd swarmed me, camera lights flashing in my face. Geoff hadn't made it to the hospital yet, so it had been a poor, unprepared nurse who'd pushed me in a wheel-chair out to a waiting car, and there wasn't a thing she could do about the horde. I'd braced myself for a question or two, but nothing like what hit me. They'd bombarded me.

How does it feel to be the only survivor, Miss St. Lyons? Like shit.

How did you manage to escape the plane and get on the seat cushion? By levitating, jerk.

What did you see when the bomb exploded? People dying, asshole.

Did you get to say goodbye to your parents? Fuck you.

"Hello? Are you still with us?" Blair smirked as she waved her hands in front of my face.

With nausea rolling around in my stomach, I bolted out the door of the Java and Me and stopped at my car, chest heaving like I'd run a marathon. I sagged against my car.

An airy voice came from behind me. "I don't mean to pry, but that Blair's a meanie who gets way too many lip injections and tummy tucks. FYI, she's older than everyone thinks. Rumor is she paid ten thousand dollars to get a fake birth certificate that makes her ten years younger, which would mean that instead of the thirty-three she claims, she's really forty-three. Which is like ancient in LA. And don't even get me started on her breast size—hello, terrifying! And totally fake. I bet she can't even sleep on her stomach, so who's the real winner there? Can you imag-ine the back pain? Or the ill-fitting bikini tops—okay maybe that part would be cool. Whatever. I prefer my B cup any day." She paused. Probably to take a breath. "Seriously, don't let her get to you."

I'd spun around to see the person who'd witnessed my fiasco. She was young, about my age, with brown hair that was pulled back with a sparkly headband. I recognized her immediately as the regular who always wore pink. She took a sip from a coffee, looking chic in a fuchsia angora sweater and white pencil skirt with a long strand of pearls draped around her neck. Three-inch white stilettos graced her feet.

She was a life-sized Hello Kitty, business version.

I blinked at the sheer pinkness of her, but then came to my senses and sent her a smile. "I know. Stupid for getting worked up about it. Maybe if I fawned over her or asked for her autograph like everyone else, she'd be nicer."

The girl agreed. "She's not nice to me either, *and* she's dating one of my clients." She added in a whisper, "Word is she's struggling for those younger starlet roles now. Her last cover for *Cosmo* was completely photoshopped. Awkward."

Wow. Pinky seemed to know a lot about Blair.

I grinned. "She's an empty-headed bubble with Manolo's and lipstick, and she needs to be popped," I said, acting it out with my fingers. "*Pop!*" Apparently, I was much braver away from Blair.

The girl's nose scrunched up as she bounced on her heels. "Yes! And she shall forevermore be known as *Bubbles.*"

I grinned. "So . . . you're in the movie business?" I asked as I relaxed against my silver Maserati.

She nodded and hurriedly fished a card from her Chanel clutch. "Mila Brady, PR person at your service. And before you say it, I know I'm young—twenty-three if you must know—but I already have a couple of big-time clients. Ever hear of the Vital Rejects? Spider—his real name's a secret—and Sebastian Tate are the front guys. Total hotties." She blushed. "I actually used to be over the moon for Sebastian back in high school—but I'm over it."

Had I heard of them? I shook my head. "If they're recent, then I'm clueless. I've been out of touch for the past year or so." Understatement. I'd been hiding out in a Hollywood mansion, refusing to see anyone.

"Oh." She looked disappointed. "Do I detect a New York accent, then? Are you an actress? You're pretty. Like really pretty. You could use a new shirt maybe though. One with more color. Just a thought." She grinned. "Sorry. I talk a lot. Sometimes it's stupid stuff, but I can't turn my brain off."

I shook my head. "No, don't apologize. Yes, I'm from Manhattan, and no, I'm not an actress. I—I'm a violinist." I said the words haltingly. It had been months since I'd talked to anyone about music.

"Cool. Why did you come to LA?"

I waffled, shifting my feet, settling with the truth. "California was as far as I could get without a plane. I recently got a job playing at an Italian restaurant, although I haven't started yet." Yep, one day you're a star violinist, the next day you're playing for celebrities sucking on spaghetti Bolognese.

"What restaurant? Are you here to make a record? Sign a deal? Are you in a band? You know, if you need help getting your name out there, I'd be glad to do the work for you. Just throwing that out there."

"It's called Masquerade."

She nodded. "Great. I'm supposed to meet up with some friends there this week—maybe I'll see you."

God, I hoped not. What if I wasn't able to play?

"I'm V by the way," I said impulsively, holding my hand out. She shook my hand. "What's V short for?"

I didn't even blink. "Just V." I didn't want her to know who I was. Not really. Not when as soon as she pieced it together, she'd get that apologetic look in her eye, and then I'd feel guilty all over again for killing my parents.

She grinned. "I'm headed down to Rodeo Drive for some errands. You wanna come with?" She bit her lip at my silence, tucking her purse up under her arm. "It's just . . . I moved here a few weeks ago, and to be honest, you're the first girl who seems like someone I could get along with." She gave me a crooked grin. "Plus, I'd love for you to meet my friends."

There were more like her? I stifled a grin.

Her offer of friendship made me waver, but I shook my head and mumbled a stupid excuse. Hanging out with her wouldn't change the fact that I couldn't have friends. It was dangerous to care for people. Something would happen to her. She'd die. Or she'd decide I was too much effort. Too strange. I didn't need anybody. I was better alone.

She gave me a disappointed smile, hopped in her little white Mercedes and drove out of my life.

Or so I thought.

CHAPTER 3

"I was sorrow with skin."—from the journal of Violet St. Lyons

A FEW DAYS LATER, I WENT FOR MY DAILY RUN AROUND SEVEN IN the morning.

I looped past *his* house as usual, noting the gray Hummer and the vintage Mustang in the circle drive. I saw something new: a white Mercedes parked to the side and facing the road, giving me a clear view of the front-end. Surrounded by pink rhinestones, *Mila* was stamped on the nameplate.

Whoa. I came to a stop at the bottom of their drive. What was she doing here this early in the morning? Of course, the implication was she'd slept over.

That thought made my stomach drop.

Was she seeing my guy?

My guy? I laughed out loud at my idiocy. I'd never even met him.

Part of me—the ballsy side—wanted to knock on his door, see what Blond Guy looked like close up, *see if he was hooking up with Mila.* Yup, crazy.

My feet had ideas too, and I took a step toward the door . . . and another . . . and then stopped.

I couldn't just show up at his door like we knew each other. Right?

Hey, how are you? I'm the girl next door. You spy on me? I gave you the finger?

Yet, I couldn't deny that he fascinated me, that the night I'd played for him it had felt as if a gossamer thread connected us, his house to mine, his eyes to my body.

I stood there, wavering. *Don't be a chicken.* Just go knock on the door.

Then what? Chew him out for spying? Ask him over for dinner?

Someone inside the house walked past a window, and my bravado disappeared.

I spun around and ran. Stupid, stupid, stupid. No way was I ever knocking on his door.

About a mile down the street, I stopped at Mr. Wilson's gate, where he stood messing with his rose bushes. He'd lost his wife to cancer about a year ago, and we'd actually met at a local grief meeting. It wasn't until later we realized we were neighbors. In his sixties, he claimed to be a simple man, but I knew at one point he'd been a Hollywood bigwig, some kind of movie studio head. Ha. At one point, I'd been on the cusp of a great music career. We had a lot in common.

He set down his shears, wiped his face and came out to the road to greet me. It was our thing, and I looked forward to talking to him. He reminded me of my dad.

I leaned over my knees to get my breath while he talked about pruning.

"You meet the new neighbors in my cove that moved in a few weeks ago?" I asked him a bit later. He was the head of the Homeowners' Association, so if anyone had info, Wilson would. I whistled and walked around his roses, like my asking wasn't completely out of the ordinary for me.

"Sure did. I stopped by the week they moved in. One's got blue hair; an English fellow. Cusses a lot. The other one, a tall guy, seems like the responsible one."

I grinned. I'd come to the right place.

"Who are they? Actors? Models? Directors? Mental institution escapees?"

He gave me a pointed look, a glint in his eyes as if he were trying to suss me out. "Why do you care so much about the new people? In fact, I've sent you several invites to our monthly pool party mixer and you've never responded. You're practically a hermit."

"Just curious. They *are* my nearest neighbors, and I'd hate to bother them if my music was too loud. I play my violin outdoors, which was fine when no one lived there, but now that someone's there . . ." I trailed off and shrugged. Obviously, I was digging a hole.

He cocked an eye at me.

I groaned. "Okay, fine, you got me. The blond guy *is* interesting. He laughs a lot, plays a guitar, and takes midnight swims if you must know. He's got nice pecs, too, not that you care to hear it. Anyway, I've never seen a girl at his house—but this morning there was a white car parked in his drive with *Mila* on the front tag. I'm guessing this means he has a girlfriend—not that I'm interested."

"Uh-huh. You thinking of opening a detective agency?" He might have been laughing at me.

I crossed my arms and fake glared at him. He grinned.

"Forget the car thing. Did you get a name? An occupation? Is he dating some chick who wears pink and looks a lot like Charlotte from *Sex in the City*?" I bit my lips to stop the madness.

He guffawed, looking pleased. "You have a crush," he teased.

I felt my face redden. *Did I?* It had been a long time since I'd been genuinely interested in the opposite sex. Not since Geoff.

"Why don't you bake them some cookies? See what happens," he said.

"I can't cook. All I have are Oreos."

"Then just show up. Smile. Make some new friends, V. I worry about you being alone all the time."

He was the only one who knew the truth of who I was. In fact, he'd met and worked with my parents on a charity benefit for the Metropolitan Museum in New York several years ago. Somehow out of all the people in LA, I'd ended up being friends with someone who'd had contact with my parents. Here's the thing, it had felt like fate, and perhaps that was why I was easy with him. Hanging on to the shreds of my past.

Wilson made a funny noise in his throat almost like a choke. His brow shot up and his eyes darted back and forth between me to something behind me. I stifled a grin, figuring it was Mrs. Milano, his fiftyish, widowed neighbor who wore her bathing suit most of the time. She must be watering her lawn again in her sparkly gold bikini. This *was* LA.

I sighed. "Anyway, back to the neighbor. He's probably a total wiener. At the very least he's a Peeping Tom—" I stopped as Wilson shook his head emphatically, eyes flaring.

I froze, except for the leg tapping. "Shit. Tell me he isn't standing behind me," I hissed.

Wilson gave me an apologetic smirk. "Okay, I won't tell you."

Dammit.

I turned.

Him.

My breath snagged in my throat. My ovaries exploded.

With impossibly broad shoulders and a jawline that could cut glass, Blond Guy grinned, his otherworldly ice-blue eyes raking over me, lingering on my pink running top. My body sizzled in awareness and my hand shot to my chest, trying to hush my heartbeat.

My telescope hadn't prepared me for the vision he made, tall with skin so sun-kissed beautiful I needed sunglasses just to peer at him.

And his sexy lips. They were way too sensual looking for a white boy.

He stood there, his stance wide and arms crossed, those big biceps mocking me with their tattoos of skulls, music notes and even a Superman emblem. I sucked in a shaky breath. Whoever this man-candy was, he belonged in the limelight where people could gaze at him adoringly.

He was trouble with a capital T and hott with two t's.

He was everything I didn't need.

We stared at each other, everything else fading into the background. Seconds ticked by, maybe an entire minute, but I couldn't let him go, taking in the way he stood there, so effortlessly, so nonchalantly, *as if he hadn't seen me play half-naked.*

Wilson cleared his throat, and we both startled.

Blond Guy stepped past me and handed Wilson a letter, his arm brushing against mine, and I hissed at the contact, tingles rushing up my spine.

He stopped momentarily at my intake and tossed me a questioning glance before he turned his gaze to Wilson. "Good morning, Mr. Wilson. This accidentally got put in our mailbox yesterday, sir. Thought I'd return it."

I stood there tapping as he and Wilson chatted. I confess I have no idea what they spoke of. It could have been as mundane as the humidity; it could have been as titillating as military secrets.

He abruptly turned back to me as if to speak, and the toe of his shoe got tangled up on the curb. He lost his balance, and I watched in fascinated horror as his body lunged toward the concrete, but at the last minute, he caught himself on the gate that led up Wilson's drive. Not as smooth as I'd thought. A weird laughter burst out of me, and I tried to reel it in. Unsuccessfully.

He straightened up, spread his hands apart and grinned manically. "Crazy, right? You called me a wiener, and I'm still falling all over you."

His easy words slammed into me, and my laughter stopped. My mouth opened.

Not only was he easily the most gorgeous male I'd ever seen, but he was disgustingly charming.

But his hotness was irrelevant.

Because I sensed a guy who crushed hearts like saltine crackers in soup.

I sensed a guy who thought he was so awesome he was fairy dust.

I turned around and ran as hard as I could, away from those eyes, that body, that smile—and that fucking perfection I didn't need.

❧

As if fate meant for us to be together, my reprieve from him didn't last long.

The next day, after my run and a hot shower, I skipped the coffee shop to avoid Blair and instead went to the ice cream shop next door that opened at eleven.

That was how I found myself trying to decide between ice cream flavors, mostly the chocolate ones. Major decisions for a junk food addict.

"May I taste the Brownie Chocolate again?" I asked the young girl behind the counter. I smiled sheepishly since I'd sampled at least ten already. She sighed heavily and left to get another spoon for me.

"You know, if it's that hard to decide, why don't you just get them all," a husky voice rumbled from behind me.

"That's thirty-five flavors. I want to enjoy my ice cream, not make myself sick." I tossed a grin over my shoulder at the mystery voice, expecting to see some dad with his kids waiting in line.

Instead, my gaze crashed into Blond Guy. I sucked in a sharp breath and all the hairs on my body rose up in unison.

A choir of angels may have sung in the distance. I told them to hush.

I stood straighter in my white shorts and Foo Fighters shirt, immediately wishing I'd put on something prettier. "Did you follow me?"

He scoffed. "No."

"So this is a coincidence? Out of all the ice cream shops in LA, you walk into mine?"

He cocked an eye. "Your gin joint, huh?"

He'd gotten my *Casablanca* reference. "I love old movies," I said.

"Me, too," he said quietly, studying me intently although I refused to reciprocate. I'd already taken a good look in those few seconds and knew he wore a Dallas Cowboys hat pulled down low, his thick hair curling up around the ends and framing his masculine face. He looked like a dessert I wanted to sink my teeth into, and I had to keep reminding myself that I was on a low calorie diet when it came to relationships.

He leaned in. "Uh, I'm glad I ran into you. I wanted to tell you I'm sorry for spying on you. It's just . . . the first time I heard you play, I wanted more. You're—"

I shook my head.

"What?" he asked.

"Don't apologize. I need to practice knowing someone sees me. Hard to explain, but I freak out when I play in public and haven't played on stage in a while."

"I'm sorry," he said as he considered me. "That must be very hard. It's brave for you to tell me."

I swallowed at the butterflies that had taken up in my belly. "Yeah, I'm not a beauty queen or a genius or an athlete, but violin was the one thing I excelled at."

"I might have to disagree on the beauty part, but regardless, I'm glad to be part of your comeback." He eased up closer and I felt his eyes on me as I tasted the sample the shop girl handed me. I shifted, moving a step back. Distance. I needed it.

He rubbed the back of his neck, a torn expression on his face. "I'm actually here to meet someone, but I've got ten minutes before she shows. You wanna hang till then? I'd love to hear more about how you got started on the violin."

She? He had a date coming?

"Can I help *you* with a sample?" Counter Girl breathed at him as she came to life and tittered behind the counter like a teenage groupie. Figures. All it takes is a muscular chest to get all the free samples you want.

He ignored her, his ice-blue eyes on me. "Well?"

"Er, I'm actually in a hurry"—total lie—"and . . ." I petered out as he suddenly grinned. "What?"

"You really have *no* idea who I am, do you?" he said softly as he leaned in my space and whispered in my ear.

My breath hitched at the swirl of air his voice created on my neck. "No. Should I? Want to fill me in?"

"Nah, I like this. No expectations. No questions."

I eyed him. "You've piqued my interest. Should I bow down?"

This time he laughed loud, the sound echoing through the tiny shop, causing more than a few pairs of female eyes to linger on him. Male, too.

He slipped on some aviators, adjusted his cap lower and shot me a cocky grin. "I'm just a simple, hot guy out for ice cream. Just like everyone else."

I laughed as he turned to the counter girl, who was currently ogling his well-developed ass. He acted like he didn't notice, ordered our ice cream, and then handed me a jumbo bowl of Double Mocha Fudge.

I took it from him with glee, taking a big bite with the plastic spoon. "I'm not sure If I should be flattered or scared that you noticed what my favorite flavor is."

"I watch you do a lot of things," he said silkily. "I watched you tap dance across your patio one day—not very well, I might add. I've also watched you gaze at the stars and write in your little notebook—which I presume is a diary." He paused. "Is it weird that I like watching you?"

"Very." But it made me hot all over. "You can't see into my bedroom can you?"

He stilled, his eyes finding mine. "No."

A shiver went over me, heat flooding my face at the intensity of his gaze. I had to look away. "I guess if you're buying me ice cream, I *could* sit with you."

"Don't act like it's a hardship," he teased as he escorted me to the back of the shop to find a table. "Millions of girls would mow you over to share ice cream with me, so sit your sweet ass down and talk to me." He pulled out a seat for me.

I sat, but rolled my eyes. "Modesty is not your forte."

"No, but honesty is. I promise never to lie to you."

Oh. His words were said lightly but seemed like a warning.

We settled in and ate our ice cream while he kept sneaking glances at me, his eyes skating over my face, lingering longer than necessary on my lips.

I licked them. "What? You're making me paranoid. Is there ice cream on my face?"

"No, it's just—you seem vaguely familiar to me. But then, I'd never forget a girl like you." He took a bite of ice cream, still scanning my face.

I didn't want him to piece it together, so I played it off. "You're dangerously smooth. My mother always said to avoid boys like you."

He snorted, his lips kicking up in a grin. "Me? Moms love me. I can cook—thanks to my big brother Leo—I like romantic movies like *Casablanca*, and best of all, I talk to my one-year-old niece on the phone every day. She's my bro's daughter and her name's Gabby, and she's the most beautiful girl in the world." He winked. "You're the second prettiest, of course."

I mulled that over, my stomach doing a topsy-turvy thing at the image of him cooing on the phone to his niece.

He cleared his throat. "So, no-name girl, I've been wondering who you are and I have some theories."

I blinked. "Yeah?"

He smiled back. "Are you an ex-porn star?"

"Uh, no."

"Ax-murderer who killed her last boyfriend?"

"No, he still lives."

He chuckled. "Then I think we're good."

"So . . . are you a famous surfer?" I asked, eyeing the shark's tooth necklace resting against his shirt.

He rubbed the necklace. "This little gem was taken from a shark the size of a bus. True, I had to kill him with my bare hands, but it's quite eye-catching. I call it my lucky necklace."

"You kill sharks in your spare time?" I could see it with those nice arms he had.

He grinned. "Truth is, I actually wore this necklace in a video I made, and it *is* lucky. Our video made us huge."

Music video? My interest was piqued, but I dampened it. "Cool."

Suddenly, he took it off from around his neck and draped it over mine, his fingers brushing over my collarbone. "Wear it for me when you play again."

A hush settled over our table at his words, and my heart took up its crazy pounding as I imagined playing for him wearing *nothing* but the necklace.

Maybe he was a mind reader because his eyes went low and he leaned in over the table. "This is going to sound crazy, but it feels like we have this thing between us—" he stopped, indecision working his face.

"Thing?"

"Never mind. It—it's stupid."

I let it go.

"Why do you do that?" he asked later, nodding his head at my tapping fingers as they beat against my thigh.

I stopped as heat washed over my face. God. I hadn't even been aware of it.

"Don't be embarrassed," he said. "It's just you did it yesterday when I saw you at Wilson's and now, so naturally, I'm curious."

"Uh, yeah. I have a tapping problem."

"Kinda like an eye twitch?" He laughed. "I get those all the time, especially when my roomie does crazy shit. Which is more often than you'd think."

I smirked. "I'd explode if I tried to stop. Mostly, it soothes me . . . kinda like a baby that sucks its thumb."

"Or a gunslinger who's getting ready to fire off a shot." He mimicked the action of pulling a gun from an imaginary belt and firing it at me.

I giggled and then cocked my head in surprise. "You're not like I expected," I said, biting my lip at the words. Maybe it was a sixth sense or a gut feeling, but I knew Blond Guy wasn't judging me for my eccentricities.

"What do you mean?" he asked.

"Well, you're overwhelmingly gorgeous—I'm sure you know that—yet you're kind. It's refreshing. Surprising even." I spilled more. "My tapping was worse when it first started—I'd get blisters on my fingers I did it so much. Some of my friends, even my ex . . . were embarrassed by it, or maybe they just didn't know *what* to say." I stared down at the table. "I appreciate you not making a big deal about it."

A gentle look came over his face as he picked up my free hand and stroked my palm. "There are worse things in life than tapping your leg. I don't know what happened to you, but I'm glad you're still here. Your tapping makes you unique. Also—" he grinned and wiggled his eyebrows "—I happen to dig *different*, Violin Girl."

A bolt of electricity zapped through my insides and went straight to my lady parts. "Violin Girl?"

Just then a commotion at the door caught his attention, and I angled my head and took in Blair Storm, sweeping inside the entrance in a tight white sundress and skinny stilettos, entourage in tow. Perfect. Guess they'd moved from the coffee shop to here. Dammit. I sighed.

Patrons pulled out their camera phones and started clicking away as she waltzed around, her mane of white hair caressing her shoulders as she pranced by like a My Little Pony. A group of young girls squealed and ran to her with paper and pen out. She obliged with a sweet smile on her face.

Only I knew better.

I wished I didn't let her bother me.

He let go of my hand and snapped up out of his seat, nearly knocking down his chair. His eyes careened from me to Blair and then back again, as if he couldn't make up his mind about what to do or say.

"What's wrong?" I asked.

He popped off his hat and ran a hurried hand through his hair. "I—I have to go. My friend's here now."

My eyes flew to Blair. "*She's* who you're meeting?" I hissed, filling in the gaps.

"Look, I wish I could explain, but it's complicated."

Disappointment settled in me, and I held my hand up. "Wait. Is she your *girlfriend*?" Maybe he wasn't the sweet person I thought he was.

He shrugged, his mouth thinning, and I waited for him to explain further, but he just stood there.

"So what you're *not* telling me is that you and her are a thing?"

He eased off his sunglasses and tucked them in his pocket with care as if weighing his words. "Do you mind if we talk about this later? I can't explain—"

"No. Just tell me the truth. Are you and Bubbles going at it?"

"Bubbles?"

I waved my hands at him. "Never mind that. Just answer the question."

"What do you mean?" He crossed his arms.

And then I started babbling. "Are you doing the bedroom rodeo with her? You know, bumping uglies? Rolling in the hay? Playing hide the sausage? Churning butter? *Making love?*"

His jawline tightened, and his eye definitely twitched. "I don't owe you an explanation of my love life. How do I know you won't spill what you know to the media?"

"I guess you don't. Maybe I like to keep my own name out of the papers. Maybe you and Blair aren't the only famous people in this room." I groaned at my own stupidity. I'd said too much. I picked up my purse, eyeing the paparazzi who'd come into the shop. They weren't here for me, and I hadn't even been on their radar in a long time, but I still wanted to avoid them.

"Thanks for the ice cream," I said tersely. "Next time . . . pretend you don't know me if we happen to see each other."

"Wait. Don't go," he said as I headed to the door.

But I knew he didn't mean it. I wasn't an imbecile. I could tell he hadn't wanted to be seen with me.

"Violin Girl!" he called out, frustration evident in his voice, but I increased my stride, anxious to put distance between us. Like an idiot, I looked over my shoulder as a soft cooing came from Blair. I watched her jump in his arms and lay a big kiss on his cheek. My stomach rolled, and I don't even know why.

I backed out the door, unable to tear my eyes off them.

CHAPTER 4

"First impression? She called me a wiener."—Sebastian Tate

"WHO WAS THAT GIRL?" BLAIR HISSED UNDER HER BREATH AS we posed for a couple of pictures inside the ice cream shop.

"My neighbor. No one that concerns you."

She reached out, her hands taking mine in a fake handhold. "It concerns us both if the media even sniffs that we aren't a real couple. You want that movie, don't you?"

I shot her a dark look. "Don't patronize me, Blair. I know exactly what I want and I'll do whatever it takes to get it. I also know you need me to make you look younger for those acting jobs you want. We both benefit."

"You seem to have the gist of it." She applied lip gloss and then puckered up her mouth. "Now kiss me. There's a guy from TMZ here."

I feigned a happy expression and took her mouth, my hands on her shoulders. Her hairspray smell clogged my nose, reminding me that she didn't smell like strawberries, like Violin Girl had. I closed my eyes and wondered what kissing *her* mouth would be like. Would her lips be as soft as they looked? Did she like long, slow kisses or hard ones that took her breath away? Would she even want to kiss me? I clenched my hands, remembering how close we'd been at our table, how I'd ached to know more about her but had sensed she needed to go slow.

And the tapping.

What had happened to her? I'd been truthful with her. Her quirk hadn't bothered me. In the big picture, it wasn't what stood out about her. Nope. What struck me were her big lavender eyes, creamy skin, and jet-black hair.

Most of all, I felt like I knew her even when I didn't.

Did she think about me at all?

The kiss ended and I pulled back to tweak Blair on the nose. All for show. She fluttered her eyelashes at me and started talking, but I barely listened, my head still running through every little second I'd spent with Violin Girl. Analyzing it. Would she play for me again? What song would she do next? I got amped up just imagining it.

Then I got pissed at myself.

Daydreaming about her was insane. Blair might be hard to deal with, but she was my ticket to the big time, and the only girl I needed to be focused on right now. My goal was not to woo the raven-haired beauty that lived next door, but to be a star.

"What would you like to eat, babe?" I asked a bit later as we stood at the counter.

"Apparently, you've already had ice cream," she snipped in a low voice. "Are you going to eat again? That's a lot of calories, Basty."

I tampered down my flare of anger. "Don't make me regret this," I said in her ear through gritted teeth. "Stop bitching and let's get this done. I have a meeting in an hour that I can't miss."

One that no one knew about.

"Fine." She shrugged.

"And don't call me any of your ridiculous nicknames. I'm not your pet."

She let out a tingling laugh and squeezed my arm as she

gazed adoringly into my eyes. "Of course, darling. Whatever you say."

I had to give it to her. She really was a good actress.

※

"Welcome to Lyons Place," said Mrs. Smythe with a flourish as she led me back to her office.

I gazed around at the orphanage, taking in the freshly painted walls in the foyer and the staff who milled around. I got a good vibe from the place, and it put a spring in my step. For once, I was doing something I wanted, not something Harry Goldberg, my new Hollywood agent, had recommended. He was all about the social aspect of my career—especially Blair—and that was essential, but I also wanted to do something that was just for me. Something relevant.

A wiry janitorial lady loaded down with cleaning supplies and pushing a mop bucket stopped me for my autograph. She fumbled around in the pockets of her uniform and pulled out a piece of notepaper. Her hands shook. "Sebastian Tate! Good God, my daughter will go nuts when she sees this. Thank you!" She beamed at me.

I signed it and handed it back. "No problem. Anytime." Feeling nostalgic, I leaned in and gave her a quick hug. Truth was she kinda reminded me of my own mom, Rachel, who'd died fifteen years ago. She'd been a hardworking lady too, spending her days at a local LA diner to contribute to the family. Dad had been a musician, and her extra tip money had come in handy.

The cleaning lady left whistling, and I followed Mrs. Smythe into her office and sat down in a leather chair. Petite and fiftyish, she sent me a cool businesslike smile. I got the impression she wasn't impressed with my star power. "Well. I was shocked to get your email and then your persistent phone messages about your interest here. It's not everyday we get requests from celebrities offering their services. Money, yes, but not their actual time, Mr. Tate—"

I sent her my best charming smile. "Call me Sebastian, please."

"Okay," she said on a blush and then cleared her throat. "To tell you about us, we're a new facility focused on the arts with a heavy emphasis on music. We house a hundred kids here, with plans to develop it further in the future."

I nodded. I'd read up on the place on the internet after I'd seen the sign going up one day on my way to the music studio. Black and gold, the signage had caught my eye because of the lion on it. He was standing on his hind legs and roaring—just like a family crest. I'd had a thing for lions since my sister-in-law Nora called me one. Long story short, she tended to match people up with animals. A lot. For example, my brother, Leo, was a tiger, Mila was a bunny, and I was the lion of the family because of my great hair and general awesomeness. I was the king of the jungle—or at least the king of Hollywood. Anyway, it was my family nickname. I even had a tribal lion tattooed across my shoulder and down my back.

She continued. "Our students—orphans—are teens. Most are from poverty backgrounds and face underlying emotional issues such as ADHD or Autism. Some even have past drug problems. Some are recently orphaned and others have been in the system since birth. I guess what I'm trying to say is each child is different and hand selected by our board of directors and benefactor, who prefers to remain anonymous." She sighed and tapped a pen on her desk. "To be honest, I am still trying to figure out what to do with you. Is there a particular reason you chose us?"

I'd gripped the chair while she talked, my past pricking at my heart. Sure the sign had captured my attention, but there was also a piece of me that remembered my own gangster neighborhood and how I'd lost my parents. That was the part of me that wanted to give back and be part of this community. I wanted roots here, and what better way than investing myself.

"Lots of reasons. I'm an LA boy at heart . . . I grew up here. When I was eight, I lost my parents to a junkie who shot them in a carjacking." I took in a shaky breath and let it out slowly, remembering the fallout from that day. "I saw it happen. I—I was on the porch waving goodbye just as they pulled out. This guy came running up—got in the car with them . . . and killed them." My throat got full, and I lifted my hands and scrubbed my face. "Sorry—for getting emotional. Sometimes it feels like it was just yesterday."

"I'm sorry," she said, her face softening. "I had no idea."

I nodded. "It was a hard time for my family, and we had some lean years until my brother Leo made money in gym ownership."

"Your story is similar to some of the kids here, Mr. Tate, except you're rich and famous now." She smiled. "Why do you think you'd enjoy helping?"

I cleared my throat, anxious to make a good impression. "People assume I grew up with a silver spoon in my mouth, but that's not the case. My brother gave up his own music career to stay with me. I remember hating him sometimes, you know, because he wasn't my mom or dad—or because all he could cook was popcorn and pizza." I laughed at those memories. "But I wouldn't be the person I am if it wasn't for him."

She gave me a considering look, mulling me over. "There's nothing like family. You're luckier than most."

"Yes."

She let out a sigh. "The truth is we're selective about who comes in to work with our kids, but I like your story—and your sincerity. I also think the kids would love to hear you speak to them—maybe play a song. We've had a few musicians come in for little concerts, mostly classical, so you'd be quite the treat."

"I'd be honored." An idea struck. "Maybe I could teach some classes on how to play the guitar—kinda like my dad taught me. Sorry if I'm being presumptuous, I'm not even a real teacher, but I think I'd be good." I leaned forward and smiled broadly. "I do have a sparkling personality, Mrs. Smythe."

She let out a laugh and blushed. Score.

I settled back. "Or, if you just need a volunteer to work the lunch line one day or clean the hallways, I'd be proud to do whatever you need." Truth.

She tapped her fingers on the desk. "Just so you know, we don't cater to the media here. No reporters are allowed inside our facility and we don't link our names with celebrities. Whatever work you do here will be confidential."

I nodded. I got what she was saying. "I don't have an ulterior motive for this. I can assure you, this isn't about me putting on a show or getting attention. This is for me alone. I could have been one of those kids."

She seemed to come to a decision about me and stood. "Great. I'll give our calendar a look and see where we can fit you in. No doubt, you're going to cause quite a stir here. I'll call you and let you know."

We shook hands and for the first time in a long time, maybe since I'd left Dallas behind all those years ago, I felt like I was *home.* I couldn't put my finger on exactly what stirred my heart—maybe it was holding Violin Girl's hand or maybe it was knowing that I was doing something worthwhile that wasn't about *me.*

Whatever it was, it felt damn good.

❧

A few days later, I woke up at one in the morning.

Violin Girl was on my mind. Constantly. She hadn't played for me since the ice cream fiasco, and frustration rode me. I'd spent three wasted nights out on the patio waiting for her to appear. Spider had even tried to get me to go clubbing with him and Mila, but I'd stayed home. Blair had insisted I take her to dinner, but I'd made up an excuse about working on some music. I was obsessed with hearing her play. Seeing her.

I thought back to the ice cream shop. There was no doubt Violin Girl had been angry with me when she stomped out. The question was—why? Was it because she was attracted to me and was jealous of Blair? Like me, did she feel the current between us—as if some invisible, electric wire connected us? I shoved a hand through my hair.

Did I want *her* or her music? I didn't know.

The sound of music caught my ears, and I immediately shot out of bed and headed for the window and pulled back the curtains. I opened the window. Shit. Had she been playing late at night so I wouldn't see her?

I picked up the binoculars from my nightstand and put them to my face.

What I saw made me groan.

Bathed in moonlight, she stood with her violin in hand. Her red robe swished around her body as she manipulated the strings with her bow. Staccato yet delicate notes reached my ears, the sound heartbreakingly beautiful as if an ethereal creature was whispering in my ear. Inhaling sharply, I strained forward, recognizing Verve's "Bitter Sweet Symphony", one of my all-time favorite songs. Her music captured me, wrapped me up, and I stood there wishing she were in front of me, wishing I could just touch her.

She angled her body to face my house, the small part in her robe teasing me. Her pale skin gleamed, the soft rise of her breasts visible. I immediately took a step back from the window. *Dammit.* I'd been deluding myself. This may have started out as music, but I realized it was so much more. Cloaked in her dark sounds, she was everything I never knew I wanted, but I didn't like how it made me feel.

Out of control. Yearning for something that wasn't safe.

Yet, as if my feet had a life of their own, they took me back to the window where I watched her end the piece with a long slow note.

She took her bow.

She flourished her hands.

I held my breath, waiting to see what was next.

She didn't tease me. She threw her shoulders back and dropped the robe, letting it pool at her feet as blood rushed through my veins. Like a beautiful, life-sized alabaster statue, she was fucking mesmerizing. My eyes went over every inch of her skin, imagining the cool air hitting her nipples, imagining that she said my name, even though she didn't even know it.

I clutched the binoculars so tight I was afraid they'd snap in two.

Naked.

Without boundaries. Without shame.

With my necklace on.

Beautiful. Defiant.

She'd *wanted* me to see her. And part of me thrilled at this little game we played.

Then she raised her head and stared across the shrubs, straight into the darkness where I waited.

She'd set out to torture me. Her breasts looked heavy as she cupped them, her fingers drifting over her tits. She tossed her head back and in my head, she moaned, imagining me with my fingers between her legs, entering her, teasing her. Lust hammered into me at the image, and I growled in my throat, hard, ready for her. I shoved my hands in my underwear and fisted my cock, but the action was cold. Empty. I wanted nothing but the kind of release that came from driving into her.

That's it. Enough.

I tossed down the binoculars and grabbed my jeans and slid them on, dashing out of the room without a shirt, although I did put my feet in flip-flops.

I ran out the back patio door and made it halfway to her house before it hit me.

What made me think she wanted to see me?

Better yet, *what was I going to do with her after I coaxed her into my bed?* There'd be a fallout because she was my neighbor; there'd be no walking away from her the next day, and the scary part was I didn't know if I'd want to.

Even though being with her might be the end of *me*.

I came to a stop, indecision riding me as I battled myself. Images of her flitted through my head, the arch of her neck, the curve of her waist, the way her hands had moved over her body—

But she was a fantasy. She could practically be in another

dimension for all it mattered. Sure I wanted to have the soulmate kind of love that Leo and Nora had—that was part of the reason I wanted a real home—but my dreams came first. Not this need for a girl.

With a groan and a few choice curse words, I spun around and headed back to the house.

I came to a surprised halt when I found Spider and Mila sitting out on lounge chairs, dressed in swimming clothes. I guess they'd come out after I left.

"Kinda late for a swim, isn't it?" I snapped.

They both startled, eyes big as I strode over and plopped down next to them. Monster immediately jumped up to lay on my chest. I scratched her on the head and sighed heavily. Maybe I needed to jump in the water. Cool off my libido.

"Never too late to hang with friends," Mila said in a cheery tone, eyeing me warily.

Spider just shrugged at me and set down his Jack and Coke, his eyes glued to the pink one-piece swimsuit Mila was sporting.

Whoa. I sat up straighter. It's like this. Mila's a straight-as-an-arrow-never-said-the-word-fuck kind of girl. She was not my style—and definitely not Spider's. She's our employee and friend, and we'd agreed a long time ago that she was off limits. In fact, Nora had promised she'd kick me in the nuts if Mila got her heart broken out here.

So why was Spider picking her up and tossing her in the pool with his hands all over her ass? She certainly seemed to enjoy it, shrieking and squirming with her arms wrapped around his neck.

My eyes darted between the two of them. *Were they—?* Nah. That was impossible. Because *if* he was messing with her—I'd fucking kill him, and he knew it.

They continued to frolic like two school kids, and I got antsy. I needed to get out of here. Get a breather. "Wanna go for a walk, baby girl?" I cooed at Monster, who'd been nipping at my fingers for attention. She gave me a doggy grin and yipped a yes.

"She never makes over me like that, and she's *my* pet," Spider called from the pool.

I grunted. Spider *had* bought her from a roadie a few years ago, but I'm the one who ended up taking care of her. I fed her, walked her, took her to the puppy salon. Hell, I'd even taken her to a movie premiere once. "You're my baby, aren't you? The only girl I need," I cooed to her as she licked my hand.

Spider climbed out, his lean body dripping water as he walked over to grab a towel. I flicked my eyes at Mila, who was still swimming. "Tell me you didn't mess with Mila." I kept my voice low.

He froze. "Sod off."

I stiffened. "Fuck you. She's too young—"

"Twenty-three, same as us."

I scowled. "I feel responsible for her. Remember the drummer she met in Austin that screwed her over? Took her months to recover from catching him with another chick. Don't be part of the problem, man."

He settled back on the lounger and reached for his drink. "Nothing's going on between us."

"Dude. It's nearly two in the morning. Nothing good happens late."

He lit a cig. "She's here because her apartment's being painted. The fumes were making her sick. I would have told you, but you were already in the bed."

If that was the whole story, then why did he keep looking at her like she was a slice of his favorite pie?

I exhaled and stood up, ready for my walk. "All I'm saying is *if* you touch her—well, then you gotta marry her or some shit."

He eyed me carefully, a hard glint in his gaze. "I don't see why you'd care. You had your chance with her and didn't take it. Do you regret it? Do you want her now?"

I groaned. "I also used to wear loafers and button-downs. Things change, but she will always be one of my dearest friends. And that means protecting her from assholes who just want to get in her pants."

He blew out a trail of smoke. "Like I said: sod off."

I snapped at his nonchalance. "Don't play with her. She deserves better."

He jerked up and glared at me with clenched fists, a red flush on his cheeks. "Why? What's wrong with me?"

My shoulders squared. Bigger and bulkier than him, I didn't doubt that I could kick his ass, but he also had the wiry thing going for him. "I didn't mean that the way it sounded, but take a good look at yourself. You drink too much, get in fights, and use girls. I don't want Mila part of that. The truth is . . . you aren't over Dovey." Dovey was his best friend at Briarwood Academy, the chick he'd loved desperately, only she'd chosen Cuba Hudson—the rich football player—over him.

I muttered, "Look, you brought up Emma and the reunion last week, but you're going to have to face Dovey and Cuba when we go back. They're going to be all over each other. Are you ready for that?"

He narrowed his eyes.

I nodded. "You're in no shape to date Mila."

His chest heaved, the veins in his neck causing his black widow tattoo to bulge. "You think I'm worthless. Just like everyone else."

45

Pain sliced through me at the hurt in his voice, and I immediately deflated. "God, no. Never. You're my number one. Me and you, we're like G-strings and strippers, beer and pretzels. Hell, you're the one who thought of us wearing the mink coats on stage. Just—she's not like the girls on the road. She's—"

"What's going on?" Mila said, coming up next to us as she rubbed a towel over her face. Her eyes went from me to Spider. "Are you two arguing?"

We gave her nothing but silence. Except for Monster. Known to be spastic, she barked at Mila and then bolted across the yard—headed straight for Violin Girl's property.

Dammit! "Come back!" I yelled as she disappeared. I sprinted after her, dodging the shrubs and evergreen trees that separated our properties. I stepped in a hole and twisted my ankle but kept going. Breathing hard and near limping, I came to an abrupt halt when I reached Violin Girl's patio area. Shock ran through me. I was exactly where I didn't need to be. Then, Monster sent me a wild-eyed look from the edge of the pool and promptly took a flying leap into the water.

Fuck.

Her head kept going under and popping back up. She was tiny—too tiny to even get out if she got to the edge. I stripped my jeans off and dove in, reaching her just as she sank. I dove under, grabbed her and backstroked to the edge of the pool. I set her down on the concrete where she immediately coughed up water, her little body vibrating. Using my arms, I leveraged myself out of the pool and picked her up. She licked me and I let out a sigh of relief. "Dammit, Monster, you scared the shit out of me."

Feeling eyes on me, I turned to face the owner of the house. She stood on her upstairs balcony, wide eyes staring as water dripped down my chest, the imprint of my male anatomy obvious from my tight black boxers. Her pool was heated—*hal-leluiah*—and my manhood stood firm. At least I wouldn't have to hold Monster in front of my crotch to hide my frozen balls.

She leaned over her ornate iron railing, her mouth a perfect *O*. She ran her eyes over my chest and abs and then to my package. Then, she clutched both sides of her robe and shoved it closed.

I grinned.

Too late, babe, I'd seen all of that.

CHAPTER 5

"This guy was some kind of dog superhero. Huh. Is there a Justice League for that?"—from the journal of Violet St. Lyons

H E BURST ONTO THE SCENE. WITH A CRAZY DOG, NO LESS. Said dog spread its legs like an Olympic ski jumper and flung itself into my pool, barely even making a splash it was so tiny. Blond Guy knifed into the water like a pro, the roaring lion tattoo on his back getting most of my attention. Dark and dangerous, the ferocious animal took up most of his back right shoulder.

My mouth gaped. Where had he come from?

Was he even real?

Had I had a few too many shots? Yes.

He rose up from his crouch, long and muscled, beads of water racing down his neck to his broad chest, calling attention to the tightly roped muscles of his abs to the delicious V of his hips. My eyes roamed over every inch of him, my mind wondering if what was under his boxers was as majestic as the rest of him.

He pushed wet hair out of his eyes, his hand continuing its journey to the nape of his neck. Then, his eyes met mine, making my stomach flutter.

I may have squeaked; I'm not a squeaker.

I clutched my robe closed, my hands tight against my chest.

"Sorry about disturbing you. Monster has dreams of being a Doberman. She won't hurt you, just likes to make her presence known."

Hurt *me*? She nearly killed herself.

"Oh? You realize it's late, right? Most dogs and humans are asleep." I pointed to the towels I'd stacked up on a shelf. "Help yourself to a towel over there. Looks like you need one."

He stalked over, moving with an easy grace of a born athlete.

Okay, play it cool. Act nonchalant. Don't say stupid stuff . . . like *wiener* or babble on about sex metaphors.

He dried the dog first, scrubbing her hair in the opposite direction and then brushing it back down. His fierce lion head tattoo winked in and out of view, its jaws open wide, the mane stretching out over his shoulder. For some reason, perhaps because this guy seemed able to pull emotion from me, his tattoo reminded me of a favorite memory. I'd always had a thing for lions, partly because our name was Lyons and it was part of our family crest, but also because of the lion at the Central Park Zoo in New York. I'd loved to hang out at his enclosure, waiting for him to spear me with those yellow eyes or chase one of his lionesses. He was majestic. He was strong. Alpha. I shivered.

I suspected Blond Guy was as well.

Finally, after what seemed liked forever of him rubbing the towel across his skin, he tugged back on low-slung jeans and re-buckled a skull belt buckle—my eyes flared at that little tidbit. He wasn't your everyday average guy.

"You dried your dog first," I said, scintillating conversationalist that I am.

"Yep."

Okay. He seemed tightlipped as well.

But then he walked closer until he stood underneath me, his eyes gleaming up at me, their pale blue color reflected in the patio lights. His gaze lingered over his necklace, and I fingered the shark tooth. I hoped he didn't want it back.

"You know, I could have shot you when you ran onto my property like that." I don't even own a gun. I didn't know what to say. My last memory of him was with Blair.

"Glad you didn't. Maybe not you, but thousands would mourn my death." He grinned. "Or would you?"

"You're an incorrigible flirt, aren't you?"

He did a snort/smirk thing. "You're a gorgeous girl—so yeah, *I was flirting*, but when you call me out like that, it kinda ruins the moment."

My lips twitched. "What's your name?" I was dying to know.

"Romeo?" His lips curled up in a grin.

"That's unfortunate."

He let out a husky laugh. "No, it's a joke, see, because the moon is out, and I'm standing here below your balcony and you're dressed—" he waved his hand at my robe "—like that. This isn't going well, is it?"

I shook my head.

"You do know the famous balcony scene in *Romeo and Juliet*, right? Shakespeare wrote it? He's kinda famous."

"I've heard of it." I kept my eye roll inside.

He took a bow. "Senior year I played Romeo in our school production to a packed house. Critics said it was the best production they'd seen in Highland Park, Texas in twenty years—although that critic may have been fourteen and wrote for the school newspaper." He shrugged and grinned. "She also had a terrible crush on me."

"Yeah?" I imagined him on stage, dressed in some type of

gold-threaded medieval outfit. "Did you wear tights?"

"My big sword made up for the girly clothes."

"Really?" I kept my eyes firmly in place, refusing to look where I knew he wanted me to. At his Big Man Stick. Because I'd noticed it already.

Straighten up, Violet! This guy was a Hollywood player and way out of your depth. "I've always wanted to see *Romeo and Juliet* on stage. I'm sure you and your sword were great."

"Well, this sure isn't Broadway, but here goes." He bent down on one knee and lifted his right hand up theatrically. He cleared his throat. "'But soft, what light from yonder window breaks. It is the east and Juliet is the sun. Arise, fair sun, and kill the envious moon which is already sick and pale with grief—'" He stopped, covering his eyes. "Ah hell, I can't remember the rest of it." He sighed. "And now the romantic moment is ruined."

I stifled my laugh.

"Technically, I make a better singer." He stood back up. "And I apologize for my poor flirting skills."

"You haven't lost your charm," I murmured.

"Thank you," he said, his gaze lingering on my face, then landing on my lips. I nibbled on them, and he froze, something primal flickering across his face.

I took a leap of faith. "My name's Violet, but I prefer to be called V."

He nodded. "I'm Sebastian, front guy for the Vital Rejects. Ever heard of us?"

Something niggled at my mind, but was I unable to figure it out. "You're part of a boy band then? Like One Direction?"

He made a choking sound. "God, no. We're rock alternative with some punk thrown in. We're edgy, not bubble gum."

"Yeah, you look more like a Kurt Cobain kind of guy."

His lips kicked up. "Yeah? You like Nirvana, right?"

He should know. He'd probably heard me play them. "He's a rock god. Once, for a contemporary music class, I redid his 'Smells Like Teen Spirit' on the violin. It was epic. My professor totally freaked out." I laughed at the memory.

Then things just kinda happened.

I leaned over the balcony, put my chin in my hand, and we began talking about music, the Dallas Cowboys football team, *The Vampire Diaries*—go figure—and just about everything we could think of.

"Here's a question for you. Do you happen to have a thing for guys with blue hair? Or do you prefer blonds?" he asked.

"You trying to fix me up with your roomie?"

"No," he growled.

I chuckled. "I guess it's more about who they are on the inside that counts." I went with my own question. "Do you like cheese puffs? Because I don't think I can be friends with someone who doesn't want to bathe in them."

"And my brain thanks you for that strange visual," he said. "My turn. Sunsets or sunrises?"

"Sunrises. New beginnings all the way."

"Me too." His eyes bored into mine.

I cleared my throat. "Wine or tequila?"

He arched a brow. "Beer?"

"Favorite color?" I asked.

"Red and lacy."

My robe was red . . . and lacy.

"Favorite movie?"

"*Star Wars*, hands down. 'May the force be with you, V.'"

"What does that even mean?"

"It means may you never be in danger. Used a lot when

fighting bad dudes with a light saber." He jumped into a fighting stance and did a few moves, and I giggled. "Come on, tell me you've seen it."

"Never."

He gaped. "I smell a George Lucas marathon. You bring the cheese puffs and tequila; I'll make sure Spider is out of the house."

Wait. *Was that a date?*

"Are you asking me out?"

"No."

Huh.

"I think you like me," I said, feeling brave.

"Sure," he said. "You're a dark-haired angel who makes her violin rock."

I nodded. "Favorite song?"

"Anything you play." He grinned. "Especially naked."

Ignore that.

"Top or bottom?" he said.

My mouth parted. "Hang on. You mean . . . sex?"

He bit his lower lip, his gaze intense. "Yeah."

"I don't know."

"Why?" His eyes smoldered.

"It's been so long . . . since, you know . . ." I trailed off.

That took him by surprise. "Lights on or lights off?"

My body burned at his questions. "At this point, I'd take either."

He groaned softly, scrubbing a hand across the faint stubble on his jaw. "Sorry. Shit. I didn't mean to go that far. Maybe we should move on."

But my heart was racing. I didn't want to stop. "Ever been in love?" I asked.

He shrugged—a good non-answer, but I saw the flash of pain on his face.

"What was she like?"

"She got pregnant. It wasn't mine." He sighed. "You ever been in love?"

I nodded.

"What was *he* like?" His eyes searched mine.

Memories from the past slammed into me—the first time Geoff and I had made love in his apartment; the day he'd given me my promise ring. I swallowed. "Wonderful. Perfect. His name was Geoff, and I tried to be wonderful for him, but in the end, I'd changed too much for us to make it."

"What changed you?"

I tapped my hands against my leg, and his eyes followed.

"It's okay," he sighed. "You don't have to explain. Maybe I've been there, too. It does get better, though—the pain. And I have a feeling life hasn't revealed its true beauty to you. You're not done yet, V."

His words.

I gripped the balcony to ground myself, to hold on to the grief that lurked inside always scratching to come out. For so long I'd been huddled in a corner, licking my wounds. I wasn't ready to come out yet. I still wanted to hide. To give up.

"You sleepy?" he asked.

I sighed. "Not even close."

He rubbed the back of his neck. "This is kinda out of the blue, but I don't wanna go home yet. Maybe you'd like to get some coffee? There's a place at the end of the canyon that stays open all night—Java and Me. We can hang out, watch the sun rise over the Hollywood sign. I've been here for weeks and still haven't done it."

"It's late," I said, the words dragging out of me. I wanted to, but it was too much, too soon.

He exhaled heavily. "Yeah, stupid idea. I didn't think it through. Forget it."

Through the open patio door, my phone rang as it sat on my nightstand. I glanced back over my shoulder, the sound jarring the silence. Wilson maybe, but he wouldn't call this late unless he had an emergency.

"Hang on a sec," I said to him and dashed inside to get my phone. By the time I picked it up, they'd hung up, but I recognized the New York number, the digits burned into my brain, into my past.

Geoff.

Feeling shocked that I'd mentioned him and then he called, my feet carried me back out to the balcony where I gingerly sat the phone down.

Had it been fate intervening?

Should I call him back?

What would I say?

How's life without me? I hear you've moved on.

"Who was that?"

I startled. I'd almost forgotten he was there.

"My ex." I stopped there, unsure how to explain that one.

"The perfect and wonderful boyfriend?" His voice had cooled. "I see. You still have a thing for him."

"No, I don't. I said *ex.* I'm not sure why he called."

"I am," he said, and muttered something about rich girls and lies and how he should have known better.

Why was he angry?

He picked up the towel he'd used and hung it over a chair to dry. "I get it. Pretty girl like you. Makes total sense for you to have a guy." He scooped up Monster, who'd been curled up in a ball sleeping.

I crossed my arms. "A guy and a girl can be friends and not sleep together."

His eyes went to half-mast. "V, I have a hard time buying that. Any guy would want you."

"Do you?"

He froze, but his eyes blazed with heat. "No."

"Then why is your chest heaving?"

My own was as well.

"Come down here, V," he said, a steely tone in his voice.

Need raced through my body, on fire to be closer to him. "Why? You could be a serial killer. And you never said you loved cheese puffs. I don't trust a man who doesn't like junk food. Plus, you're mad. Not sure I like that."

He grimaced. "I'm sorry for being an ass. I blame it on my shitty experiences with girls. Just—I don't know—come down here and look me in my eyes."

"Why?"

"Maybe I want to kiss you," he said softly.

"You're kinda bossy. And I might have whiplash from the way you go from hot to cold."

He said, "I quoted Shakespeare to you. I've never done that for a chick before. And you turned me down for coffee. First time ever. My ego took a hit and needs some stroking."

I rolled my eyes. "Fine. Thank you for the soliloquy. Next time try to remember all your lines."

He shook his head, all teasing gone. "Thank me down here. Please."

Okay, first he was all flirty, then pissy because of the phone call, and now I had no idea what was going on. But I was drawn to him with a recklessness that seemed to throw all caution to the wind.

"Give me a sec."

I turned and bolted straight to my bathroom where I flung open the cabinet, swallowed down some mouthwash, yanked the ponytail out of my hair, and put on lip gloss. Obvious much?

I zipped down the stairs, making myself slow down as I opened the downstairs patio door and stepped outside. Breathless, I took a few big gulps. Be cool.

I marched up to him, stopping just shy of his bare chest. I tilted my head up to gaze into his eyes. "Hi."

He blinked down at me, as if trying to clear his head. "Hi."

I smiled at the shyness in his voice. "I'm here," I said.

"You let down your hair." He sounded dazed. Winded.

"Yeah." I touched it self-consciously, twisting a strand around my fingers. I felt fourteen all over again and Bobby Malone was about to kiss me in a game of spin the bottle. "I swallowed some mouthwash too."

His eyes went low. "Because you thought I might kiss you?"

"Aren't you?"

He thought about it, his hand coming up to cup my cheek, the heat of it making me sway into him. He smelled like the sea, like the summer vacations my parents and I used to take at our weekend house in the Hamptons, where I'd wade my feet in the surf while my parents walked on either side of me, watching the sunset over the Atlantic.

I hadn't even known it then, but those were the happiest moments of my life.

He smelled like that. Happiness. Fairy Dust.

And with that thought, part of me wanted to retreat. To run back into the house far away from his magic.

But I couldn't. Something about him had me transfixed.

He leaned his head down, his lips close to mine. The heat from his body seared me, and I inched toward it. And just when I thought he was going to take my mouth, he stopped. "I can't kiss you until you tell me who Geoff is."

"He's not here, I know that."

He studied me. "You're thinking about him, aren't you?"

"Not even close."

His other hand cupped my cheek, his voice gentle as falling rain. "I don't like this dude very much. Can I kick his ass for you?"

Oh. He was being protective. He thought I was hurting because of a guy.

"Geoff didn't hurt me, okay? If anything, I hurt him."

He mulled that over, processing it, surprise flickering across his face "Fine. But *I* do have the potential to hurt you."

"Let me be the judge. I'm game for you to kiss me. Right here, right now. Trust me, my therapist will be thrilled. Maybe even give me a discount next time I go in."

"I'm not sure if I can stop if I do."

I scowled. "Is this my punishment for turning you down?"

"V, I can think of several ways to punish you *creatively*, and not kissing you is not one. It's punishment for myself. I—I've made a promise to myself that I won't get involved with anyone."

I closed my eyes briefly, hiding my disappointment from his searching eyes. "Fine, but if we did—kiss—what do you think it would be like?"

He traced my mouth with his finger. Gentle-like, his thumb pressed on my lower lip, and my tongue darted out to taste his skin. He watched my lips, his own parting.

"What are you thinking?" I whispered. I was thinking of

him coming into my house with me.

"That *if* we kissed, you'd bring out the animal in me, and I'd die to taste every single inch of your softness with my tongue. And not just your mouth. I'd want my lips all over you. I'd lick every corner and crevice. I'd want to eat you raw, consume you until there was nothing left."

I shivered.

That was . . . that was. Hot.

Before I could change my mind, I tilted up my head, stood on my tiptoes and kissed him. Just a press of my lips against his pillowy ones. Soft. Tentative. My hands went to his broad shoulders, easing up to the nape of his neck.

He froze, not kissing me back but not pushing me away.

Mortified, I stepped down and stared at the ground. Anywhere except at him. Heat rushed to my face. I counted my toes, noting that the red color on my nails needed to be redone. My hands went crazy against my leg.

How could I have been so stupid?

"V."

Retreat, retreat, my head said. I gave him my back, forcing my hands to be still.

"V?"

His hand cupped my shoulder and turned me around. "Look at me."

No.

"Come on, look at me," he whispered.

I sighed heavily and gazed at him. "I'm sorry."

His eyes burned into me. "No, *I'm* sorry."

"For what?"

"For this," he said, wrapping his arms around my waist and tugging me until our chests crushed together. Then his head lowered and his mouth took mine, and there was nothing tentative about it as our tongues tangled together. Immediately, every inch of my skin flared to life. Heat. Fire. I strained toward him as if I needed him to breathe. His full lips razed mine like a man starved, devouring me with each little nip and groan that came from him. He picked me up off the ground, his arms molding me to him. He was a lusty kisser, a man who took what he wanted, who pillaged. Every atom, every molecule inside me ached to inhale him, to swallow him whole and never let him go. I imagined him as a demanding lover, one who took what he wanted as hard as he wanted, but then gave you back a thousand fold. He was exactly what I needed, and I moaned out his name, and he answered by whispering mine, his hands drifting down to my collar to push inside my robe. *Yes.* I wanted his naked flesh against mine. I wanted him to sink into me and take me hard, drive away the pain of my past and make me feel good. Happy.

I don't know how long we kissed, but I burned the moment into my head, part of me afraid he would disappear, be yanked from me like everything else. I gripped his hair, my fingers threading through the strands, holding on. It may have been a kiss, but it smacked of more, of something so real I could reach my fingers out and touch it.

"V," he whispered, his voice rough like it had been dragged over gravel. "I can't stop."

"Then don't."

He moved without taking his lips from mine, guiding me until my back was pressed against the brick of the house. I parted my legs and he settled in the middle, his kisses becoming softer. Gentle. I ran my hands over his naked chest, my fingers playing with the soft skin of his nipples. He came up for air, his hands cupping my face like I was a piece of fragile glass. He looked wild, his face flushed, lips swollen, and I wanted to bite them they looked so good. I wanted affirmation I was alive. That he was right here in front of me.

"You taste like strawberries," he whispered as he kissed his way down my neck, sucking on my collarbone.

"Lip gloss," my strangled voice managed to get out.

"Mmmm," he said, spreading apart my robe and gazing down at my naked breasts. "I say we take your lip gloss and put it everywhere. Your neck, your breasts, your nipples, behind your knees, on your thighs—"

I moaned and nibbled on his lips. "Yes, it's been so long."

He stilled. "How long?"

"Two years . . . not since Geoff." Not since the crash.

He sucked in a sharp breath. "Why?"

I swallowed. "Because it hurts to care. People always leave." Or die.

He set me down gently, took a step back and scrubbed his face, frustration evident in the way he looked at me.

"What's wrong?"

He paced around the patio. "This—" he motioned between us "—is a mistake."

What?

He groaned. "Don't you see—you're in a fragile place right now, and I'd just end up hurting you too, V. I don't want that."

Hurt and then anger flared. He'd brought back my music— but he didn't want *me*.

He splayed out his hands. "Look, this is my fault. I just came over to get Monster. Not this."

My chest got tight. "You should leave," I said, pulling my robe together.

He inhaled a deep breath, his eyes seeming to plead with

me. "I'm sorry, V. Promise you'll play for me again. Hearing your music, watching how you let go—it reminds me of how I used to feel when I first discovered music. The emotion in you is so fucking visceral—"

"Stop, with your compliments. You don't have to explain."

Still he didn't move, frustration flickering across his face as he ran a hand through his hair and then tugged on it as if he needed grounding. "V?" He sounded confused. "There's something between us—I don't know what—but it scares the hell out of me. My life . . . it's crazy right now . . . and my ex got pregnant with another guy's baby, and it messed with my head—"

"Just go. Please." My voice cracked. Here I was, a silly girl who stupidly thought he was going to be the one who made me whole. Hadn't I learned that no matter how many changes you make in your life—changing your address, dumping your boyfriend, or calling yourself by a new name, *nothing ever changes.*

Grief will always keep me a prisoner.

Still he stood there, his gaze darting around my face as if looking for an answer.

I gave him one. I pivoted and walked back into the house. I clicked the lights off and went to bed. He might be a rock star, but I was Violet St. Lyons and no one kissed me and said it was a mistake.

CHAPTER 6

"Romeo was an idiot. He met Juliet, fell in love, and got hitched two days later."—Sebastian Tate

THE NEXT DAY, I STOOD AT THE DINING ROOM WINDOW, WATCHING as V jogged past the front of my house. Walking away from her the night before had been hard, my body screaming for me to take what she'd been offering. Maybe I could have kept it casual, but my gut knew that once I let myself go with her, I wouldn't be able to control getting in deep. Spider had been right. She *was* the first girl in five years who'd gotten my attention. Sure, I'd dated lots of girls, but none of them had been serious girlfriend quality, and that had been on purpose. V was everything I didn't need right now. Relationships were all about the timing, and right now sucked.

She came to a stop just outside the gate to our house. I watched as she paced back and forth for a few moments, a little crease of concentration on her face as if she were debating. Finally, she came to a decision, swung her legs over our gate and then proceeded to march straight up our drive. I grinned but then quickly frowned. It wasn't a good idea to have her here. My resolve was weak. I still remembered how she'd felt pressed against my chest, her tongue in my mouth, her hands clutching me. I groaned.

Spider stumbled groggily into the marble tiled entry, blue hair sticking straight up from his pale face. We'd had some words last night about Mila, but our spats never lasted long. They'd both been gone last night when I'd returned.

"Rough night?" I asked.

"Maybe." He scratched his crotch through his dark blue boxers. Nice.

The doorbell went off and he flinched at the sound.

"Bloody hell, who's here this early?" He stalked to the door to check the peephole. Seeing who it was, he tossed a smirk over his shoulder at me. "Now that's a sight for red eyes. It's your girl from next door."

"Not my girl," I said. "You handle it. I have some muffins to check on anyway." I left him in the foyer and headed down the hallway to the kitchen.

He snorted, yelling at my retreating back, "You're kidding me, right? There's a hottie on our steps, and you don't want to invite her in? Maybe she brought us an apple pie."

"You hate apple pie," I called back.

He muttered loud enough for me to hear. "Be warned, I never turn down girl pie."

Whatever. I kept walking until I was in the kitchen. I pulled out the blueberry muffins, and Monster flew into the room, practically salivating.

I strained to hear what Spider had decided to do, and was rewarded when I heard him open the door. Muted conversation and then laughter reached my ears. A bolt of unwanted jealousy hit me. Of course they'd hit it off.

Spider sent me a smug-ass look as they entered the kitchen together. "Look who's here," he announced. I definitely detected glee in his tone.

She set down a purple dog collar on the granite countertop, a rhinestone nameplate dangling from the center. "I wouldn't have come by so early, but I found this at the bottom of the pool when I cleaned it this morning. Thought you might need it since Monster likes to run off."

"Thanks." I did my best to not let my eyes rake over her, but they had a life of their own. I took in her tight running shirt, gray pants, and athletic shoes. Sweat still glistened on her face, and her ponytail was damp. I wanted to lick her neck and taste the salt on her body. I wanted to pull her hair down and run my hands through it. I wanted to peel her shirt off—*stop!*

She rocked on her heels a bit, looking uncomfortable as we made eye contact.

On the other hand, Spider seemed bushy-tailed, leaning against the stainless steel fridge, watching us both with a crazy glint in his eye.

I cocked an eye at him. "Don't you think you need some pants?"

He sent me a wry grin. "No way am I budging from this kitchen. Does my lack of attire bother you?" he asked V with a formal flourish.

She chuckled. "I suppose all your important bits are covered, and I love your accent, by the way. It makes your near nudity quite funny."

He barked out a laugh and stuck his hand out. "Great. I'm Spider, by the way. I think I missed saying that at the door. Probably because I was blinded by your beauty."

"I'm V." Her eyes lingered on his tattoos. She smiled at us both. "So. You got any bananas?"

"What's going on?" I asked as Spider handed her a couple of bananas from the fruit stand on the counter.

"When I opened the door, V noticed how poorly I looked and offered to make me a hangover remedy. By the way, nice of you to tell me you took a swim in the neighbor's pool to rescue Monster."

"I didn't tell you because you were gone when I got back," I snapped, jealous of their instant camaraderie.

"I'll need more fruit—whatever you have. And something green, like spinach or kale or fancy lettuce," she said, busily peeling the bananas and ignoring us. "Oh, and a mixer or a blender would be great, too."

I found the blender while Spider pulled oranges and spinach leaves out of the fridge. "This work?" he said.

"Perfect," she said brightly, taking it from him. "Once you drink this, you'll be ready to take on the world."

"Healthy drinks aren't my cup of tea, but I'll try anything for you." He smiled broadly, his eyes crinkling in the corners. *Great.* He liked her—which was a rarity.

I grunted.

She shot me a look. "You need one too? It'll help."

"With what?" I muttered.

"With your grunting problem. Constipated?" she asked.

Spider snickered. "Oh, he's just mad because I let you in."

"Is that so?" she said, giving me a careful look.

"We left on weird terms last night," I admitted.

"What happened last night?" Spider chimed in, eyes darting between us.

"Nothing," V and I said in unison.

He narrowed his eyes. "Uh-huh."

I checked out the mixture she'd put in the blender. It looked disturbing, but I held my tongue. I smiled. "So I take it you like to cook?" Being cool. Pretending like I didn't want to sweep her out of this kitchen and straight to my bed.

She laughed. "Don't let my expertise with fruits fool you.

I'm a lousy cook. On the other hand, if you like cheese puffs and Oreos, I'm your girl."

"I love Oreos," Spider said in a flirty tone, and she rewarded him with a smile.

"Here, peel those," she said, tossing me an orange.

"This is going to be gross, isn't it?" I asked as she poured ice water over the mixture.

She shook her head. "My mom used to make these when I was sick with a cold. She swore it cured whatever ailed you."

"Yeah, because it made you sicker," I joked.

"Funny," she said and hit the button, turning the contents a greenish-brown. Spider pretended to throw up in his mouth.

"You see your mom often?" I asked.

She went white and her hands stilled as she lifted the blender off the base. "She's dead. Both of my parents are."

My chest constricted at the pain on her face. "Recently?"

She nodded, and I noticed she was gathering herself, her throat muscles working as she swallowed. And right there in the kitchen with the early morning sunlight shining through the window, V became more than just a girl I was attracted to. She was *real*, a person who'd seen the loss of a parent at a young age, who'd faced empty chairs at the dinner table. *Like me.*

I got some glasses down from the cabinet, and she divided the green stuff between us. It sloshed into the glasses with a thud.

"You know, maybe I don't need this. I feel better all ready," Spider said uneasily as he stared at it. I bit back a grin because his face was almost the same color as the drink. Spider might be an abrasive bastard, but his stomach was as delicate as a newborn's.

"Drink it," she ordered him with a smile, and for a second I thought he might resist, but he took a small test sip.

I chugged mine to the last drop. "Excellent," I lied. No way was I going to ruin her memory of her and her mom's thing.

She leaned over to encourage Spider, and I got antsy. Did I notice that his eyes were glued to her rack? Maybe. Did I notice that she ran her eyes over his bare chest more than once? Yeah.

I set my glass down sharply. "How'd you end up in LA?"

"Lots of reasons. Mostly to get out of New York."

"Is that where your ex is?" I tried to sound smooth.

She blinked. "Yes."

Good, he was thousands of miles away. I nodded. "How's the playing coming? Any closer to getting yourself on a stage?"

Fear flickered over her face as she fiddled with her glass. "I have a job coming up, but I'm not sure I can do it."

"Maybe you could play with us sometime?" I said. "We practice a few days a week at a studio on Melrose. You could even ride with us down there." *Dammit.* Even though I didn't mean to, I was sending mixed signals.

Spider's eyes had widened at my offer. Girls were generally not allowed at our work sessions. I ignored his searching looks.

"I'll think about it," she said, but I could tell by how stiff she'd gotten that the thought terrified her. She checked her watch. "I have to go. I have an appointment later."

She was running away. Part of me was glad, but the insane side of me wanted her to stay. I let out a sigh. "Sure, let me walk you to the door."

She said her goodbye to Spider, and we walked to the foyer where I asked for her phone. She handed it over, and I typed in my digits.

"What are you doing?"

"Putting my number in so you can call me if you ever need anything. That's a big house you live in. It worries me."

She stared at me. "I think you made it quite clear last night that it's not a good idea for you to be alone with me at my house."

I groaned at the memory. "I'm sorry for kissing you and then pushing you away. I never should have let it get that far."

She nodded and stared at the ground. "No, it was my fault."

"No, it was mine. I *had* to kiss you. I wanted to since the ice cream shop."

She sent me a sly smile. "Well, if you change your mind about some super-hot-no-strings-attached-sex with me, I'm ready—" She burst out laughing. "I'm kidding. Oh my God, if you could see your face right now. It's bright red and I swear some sweat just popped out on your forehead."

"You're a little devil," I muttered and turned to the side— trying to hide my erection.

"Or a very good tease," she said softly.

I licked my lips. "Do you want to spend the day with us? Maybe drive out to Malibu and catch some rays?" I had plans with Blair, but I'd chuck them.

She bit her lip and shook her head. "Maybe next time," she said as she slipped out the door.

I watched her slowly disappear down the drive as Spider walked up behind me.

"You been lurking back there, listening?"

"You know it," he said. "This is the most excitement we've had in this house since Monster rolled in her own shit and we had to take her to the puppy salon."

I chuckled at the memory. "Poor thing. She was terrified of the blow dryer."

"And the pink hair bow they put on her—bloody ridiculous. Her name *is* Monster."

My eyes followed his to V. "Stop looking at her ass," I said, trying to edge him out of the door as we jostled for the best view. Like kids.

He sent me a calculating look. "You missed it at the door when she said she liked my hair. I think I love her."

"Stay away from V." I'd tensed up. I wasn't kidding anymore.

"Why? Maybe she wants to get on the Spider train. You aren't interested in her—are you?"

"No," I bit out, my jaw clenched.

"Bollocks. You're a liar."

I glared at him. "I can't date anyone right now. Not with the media breathing down my throat, expecting to see me with Blair. I made a deal with her, and I can't just break it off. It would cause a shitstorm of negative publicity."

He rolled his eyes. "Okay, okay, I get it. But V's the kind of chick that won't stay single for long. And those eyes? I mean you could drown in them. Like fucking pansies."

"Coming from the guy who only notices tit size?"

He cocked his head. "Maybe with her, I'd do it different."

My hands fisted. When it came to V, something in me was wired to explode. I wanted to pound his face. "*No joke.* Stay away from her."

Spider took a sip of his coffee, all Mr. Cool to my hothead. "She cares about people. You can tell by the way she waltzed in here and wanted to make me feel better."

"Yeah? You know what else I noticed about her? She's rich. And she has an ex-boyfriend who's calling her. That remind you of anyone?"

"She's nothing like Emma. First of all, cock sucking isn't her primary talent. Second, V's classy. Emma is nothing but a Dallas debutante with a hard-on for diamonds and social standing."

I tried to tune him out. But it's hard to tune out a blue-haired

English dude in his underwear. "She could be *the one* for you," he said, his tone serious.

The one? I reared back. His hangover had addled his brain. He didn't sound like Spider at all. "Since when did you get all mushy?"

"Dammit, maybe you're rubbing off on me," he snapped and then stalked off to get dressed.

Okkaaay.

CHAPTER 7

*"I'd dropped out of college, had never had a real job, or even had a
good orgasm. I didn't know jack, but I did know that even after the
people you love are torn from you, time keeps beating away at the
black metronome that's called life. It doesn't care that you've cracked
wide open, that you're screaming for everyone to just stop. It doesn't
hear you. You are nothing. People still go to dinner, planes take off
and land, lions roar, violins play. And you are left in your corner,
hanging on to memories, nothing more than a speck of dust on the
metronome's base."*—from the journal of Violet St. Lyons

T HE PLANE TWISTS IN THE SKY, SPINNING LIKE A BALLERINA.
We fall and crash into the ocean.
I scream as my neck snaps forward.
Water fills up the gaping hole on the side of the craft.
*My mother looks at me with sightless eyes. My father is gone from
his seat.*
Fear claws at me as I unclick and fight my way out of the hole.
*I turn and watch the plane sink until it's nothing but a white
speck being swallowed by the sea.*
My heart slams against my chest. Air. Lungs screaming.
Daddy. I kick harder.
Water and silence surround me.
I'll never make it to the surface.
I inhale, sucking down water that sets my throat on fire.
Someone touches me, pushes me, begs me.

Again and again I swallow until I am nothing.
I am dead.

Gasping, I woke up from my afternoon nap and kicked out, legs fighting the sheets. My body shook violently, adrenaline pounding through my veins. Clutching my rolling stomach, I sucked air in through my mouth. My hands pressed against my eyes as I called out to a deaf God to make the nightmares disappear.

I raced for the bathroom, falling on top of the toilet and retching as my fist pounded the tile floor. I vomited until there was nothing left in me but memories, little pricks of pain that festered inside, refusing to let go. I collapsed on the cold floor, tucking my knees up to my chest as I rocked myself.

When would this end?

An hour later, I sat in Dr. Cooke's office for our weekly appointment. In her forties and stylishly dressed in a pale blue pantsuit, Wilson highly recommended her as a therapist. I'd been coming here for over a year.

"How are you feeling?" she asked me as I sat in a comfy chair next to her desk and crossed my legs.

"Old as dirt. I see people my own age and want to remind them that the grim reaper can pluck them up whenever he feels like it and yank it all away. On top of that, I'm sick of being afraid to stand up for myself." I laughed at a distant memory. "When I was a kid, I punched Dougie Lombardi in the nose for trying to look up my skirt on the playground. I got an after school suspension for that one, and now look at me—I can't even tell a girl at the coffee shop to fuck off after she insults me. I'm just—pathetic. I hate it."

She nodded and tapped her pencil on her pad. "Conflict is a trigger for you. If a situation makes you uncomfortable, you want to withdraw and disengage. But you can't cocoon yourself forever—not if you want your old life back. You have to be willing to take chances again."

She was right, but admitting I needed to change was easy. Living it was the hard part.

I stood to pace around her office. Feeling fidgety. I came to a stop at the window and peered down below. Everyone looked busy. Happy. I watched a young couple hold hands as they crossed the street and found a table at an outdoor patio. Loneliness settled in my gut.

What was Sebastian doing? Was he with Blair? What was going on with them? When he'd pulled away from our kiss, *she* hadn't been the reason why. What was he not telling me?

"Any more suicidal thoughts?" She always asked that one.

I sighed. "Not in a while, no."

"Have you tried the new breathing exercises we talked about?"

Like a million times. "Yes. One long breath in and a longer one out." I tapped my leg. "Speaking of heavy breathing, remember the guy who moved in a few weeks ago? I—I've played for him." I left out the whole part about catching him spying, stripping for him, and the tequila. I didn't think she'd approve of my methods.

Her eyes widened. "That's wonderful progress, V. How did this happen?"

I shook my head. "I don't know. He's probably the next big thing in Hollywood, but that isn't the reason. It's like something in me just *clicks* when it comes to him. He gets me and he loves music, and it makes me feel the music again." I twisted my hands together. "There's more. We kissed, and I—I wanted to go further. What do you think that means?"

She blinked and adjusted her glasses. "That you're ready to move on. You've been an island unto yourself for two years, V. You need people." She smiled. "Are you falling for him?"

Was I?

"It doesn't matter. He's unavailable," I muttered.

Moving on, I described the details of my new nightmare. "Anyway, it was different this time. Someone in my dream *pushed* me toward the surface. He—a man—helped me in the water. It's odd that I've never remembered that before." Emotion welled up, and I plopped back down in the leather chair. "I can't recall how I got on that cushion and most days I wish I hadn't. But— what if—what if my dad put me on that cushion? I was swimming toward him when I blacked out. What if he was there the whole time, and I never knew it? If that's how it happened, then why did he let go? Why didn't he hang on?" My voice cracked.

She nodded. "It's possible your subconscious is telling you more of what happened—perhaps because you played for your friend. This is good." She continued. "About your dream, you might need to consider that the cushion was too small for two people or he was exhausted after getting you there. Your father was in his sixties, V. It must have been difficult for him to swim in the freezing water."

I sucked in a shuddering breath. Her words were like knives to my heart. My parents had been elderly—I'd actually been an IVF baby after years of them trying.

"But, I wanted to save *him.*"

"Don't you think he'd sacrifice his life for yours?" she said softly. "As a parent myself, I'd do whatever it took to make sure my child lived—even put her on a cushion and let go."

I sat there and wept as realization dawned. I'd been selfishly wishing I was dead along with them, when *he'd saved me and then let me go.* I didn't know why, but somehow I knew it was true. Excruciating pain sliced through me at the image of him sinking below the waves, yet at the same time, hope bloomed.

He'd given me another chance at life.

He'd wanted me to live.

When was I going to start?

᛫

Later that day, the florist delivered an extravagant flower arrangement to my house.

My foolish heart soared thinking they were from Sebastian, but they weren't.

They were from Geoff. First the phone call and now flowers—did this signal something new for us?

I stared at the pink tiger lilies and gardenias that took up most of the vase amid little spurts of greenery. Beautiful and exotic, the flowers permeated my entire house, smelling of New York and the memories of a lighter girl who'd had the world in her hands.

I set it out on the balcony and stared at it. I read and then re-read the cream-colored expensive card that arrived with it. *Missing You* was all it said on the front with a picture of two cuddly teddy bears holding hands. I grinned because it was so odd to see something as cheesy as this from him. Older than me by three years, Geoff was a law student at NYU. He was also the Mayor of New York's son. Auburn-haired and a bit stuffy, we'd fallen in love the summer I was seventeen and he was twenty. I'd never gotten what he saw in a music geek like myself when he had plenty of college girls to choose from, but he claimed he'd been in love with me since we were kids and our parents had taken vacations together.

On the inside, he'd written,

Dearest Violet,

I've been trying to call you, but you never answer. I need to see you. I'll be in LA this weekend, and it would mean the world to me—everything—if we could talk. Please make plans to see me. I miss you terribly, and there isn't a day that goes by that I don't think of you.

All my love,

Geoff

All his love?

I laughed at that. I didn't think so. I'd kept up with him in the papers and online. In the past two years, I'd seen the girls he'd dated, confident socialites with pretty dresses and even fancier college pedigrees. So what if that would have been me two years ago if my parents hadn't died. But, I was different now. Changed. The Violet who'd emerged from the Atlantic Ocean was not the big-eyed girl he'd fallen in love with.

But I didn't fault him for moving on. As he should have.

I flipped the card between my fingers, cement in my stomach at the thought of facing him again. The last time I'd seen him had been six months after the crash when I'd sat across from him at a fancy Manhattan restaurant and gone through the motions of being normal. That night, his hands had hovered constantly over me, almost as if by touch he could help me. Looking back now, I'd been too self-involved with my grief to see that he needed something I couldn't give. He'd been too focused on saving me to see that I needed to be as far from my old life as I could get.

He'd picked up my hand, his fingers toying with my

promise ring. A one-carat, princess cut diamond with emeralds on the side, it had cost more than most engagement rings. He'd smiled at me. "I know this is fast, but what do you think about a Christmas wedding? We could go to Hawaii for the honeymoon, or St. Tropez? I know how you love the sun."

The room had spun. Walk down the aisle in front of the media and all our friends? *Get on a plane?* "What?"

"I'm ready for you to start living again, Violet."

I stared at him. In horror. *Didn't he get it?* My parents were at the bottom of the Atlantic. My music was gone. I considered killing myself each day.

"You need to move on, Violet." Now, his voice was stern, and I saw him then. I saw how he was tired of my moping. Tired of my depression. He wanted his happy girl back.

I stood, my hands tapping. I was screwed up, and he had no clue because his life was still wrapped in fairy dust.

"I can't," came out of me. "I—I'm sorry."

I twisted the ring off my finger. "This piece of jewelry is the only thing that survived the crash. I lost my parents, my violin, all my luggage, even the clothes they found me in were later thrown away . . . everything is gone except this one thing." I placed it gently on the table and ended the final chapter. "And now it's gone. Goodbye, Geoff."

❦

Phil, my new boss at Masquerade, was a real ass-hat.

I should have known it from the interview when his eyes never lifted above my neck, but the needy musician in me had ignored it. Of course, he had hired me without actually hearing me play or knowing my full name, so I guess my boobs had come in handy for that at least.

He smirked as he stood up from behind his desk and adjusted the waist of his slacks. Judging by his gut, he liked to eat, and even from here I could smell the garlic and cheesy bread on his breath. "You look pale," he noted, "and lose the jacket and unbutton the top two buttons on your dress. This isn't a nunnery; it's a restaurant with a night club downstairs, so get with the program."

Keeping my face placid, I did as he asked and undid some of the buttons. Silky and fitted with a lace overlay, I'd picked the dress up today after I'd left Dr. Cooke's office. It was just the little confidence booster I needed to encourage me to get out there on that raised dais in the center of the restaurant and play. I sucked in a breath. *I could do this.*

"You busy later?" Phil asked as we left his office and walked out into the restaurant.

"Yes." If you count watching *Glee* re-runs.

He gave me a smarmy smile and licked his lips, his eyes honed in on my cleavage. "You sure? I just got a new Lamborghini. We could take a drive up to Mulholland and I could show you the sights."

"That's okay. I have a Maserati. It knows the way."

He gave me a sharp look. "Watch yourself, V. I don't like smart-mouths."

I blinked. Had I been a smart-ass? Maybe. I grinned and clung to the brave feeling that bubbled up. I tried it on for size. "Are you sexually harassing me? Because if you are, I've always wanted to own an Italian restaurant." Not true.

He puffed up his chest and took two giant steps back from me as he held his hands up in front of him. "I was just making conversation. No one is harassing you here." He cleared his throat. "Now, get over to the hostess stand and wait for me to call for you."

He marched off in a huff, and I mentally cheered. It was a tiny victory.

I headed to the coat check to hang up my jacket.

A young, female voice spoke from behind me. "*Pssst, V.*"

I looked behind me and saw the redheaded hostess girl I'd met earlier. She waved and smiled broadly from behind her stand. It was hard to believe we were the same age.

"Yeah?"

She smacked her gum. "Come over here. There's a guy in the VIP section who's staring at you like you're on the dessert menu. His eyes followed you all the way out of Phil's office. Weird, huh?"

I harrumphed. "He probably just has gas."

"He was staring so hard I'm surprised you couldn't *feel* it." She wiggled all over.

I glanced down at my black ensemble. "He's probably wondering why my dress is unbuttoned to my navel." I buttoned it back up. Screw Phil.

Her eyes flared big as saucers as she arched her neck to get a better view of him. "OMG, get this: he's with Blair Storm, which means it's *him*." She flapped her arms around.

I walked closer. "Um, you okay?" Maybe I should have applied at the Macaroni Grill down the road.

Then alarm bells rang. "Wait. Blair Storm?"

"Uh-huh," she said as she covertly held her phone next to a menu and snapped pics. "They are so freaking beautiful. My roommate is going to *die* when I text her this."

Dread pooled in my stomach. I scanned the tables hurriedly, but didn't see them. "Where?"

She pointed and I found them at a big curved booth in the back with several other people. My heart jumped as Sebastian's intense eyes met mine. His muscled arms flexed, calling attention to his hands—which were on top of the table cuddling with Blair Storm's.

Oh. I looked away, surprised by how much it hurt to see them together.

Phil walked up to the stand and clapped his hands. "Quit gawking at the celebrities with your mouth open." He looked at me. "Are you ready to play?"

My chest tightened and my eyes bounced around. I landed on Sebastian. "There's someone I have to say hello to first."

"Who?" he and the hostess girl said at the same time.

"Ahhhhhh." I nodded my head in Sebastian's direction. "Guy at table eight?"

She grabbed her chest. "You-you *know* him?"

"He came over one night to go swimming. Saved a dog. Quoted Shakespeare to me."

"OMG, you're going to be so famous," she exclaimed. "Please, get his autograph for me when you go over there. And Spider's too." She closed her eyes, in the throes of a star-gasm. "'Superman' was like the best song ever. In the video, they danced in these fur coats during a snowstorm on a rooftop . . . only at the end, you see, they take off the coats, and they're wearing these tiny bikini briefs, you know like the Europeans wear, and you can tell they have big cocks—"

I held my hand up to stop the madness. "I get the picture." I'd actually seen the famous video today when I'd googled them, but it had been their music that I'd noticed. It was wild and raw with lyrics straight from the heart. Toss in how gorgeous they were, and it was no wonder they'd hit it big.

Phil put his hand on my arm. "We don't flirt with the guests."

I shook him off. "It would be rude to ignore him—and he's waving me over." He totally wasn't, but before I could change my mind, I grabbed the note pad the hostess thrust in my face and went for it.

Anything to get my mind off playing.

I made my way over to the VIP section.

Just say hi. That's all. Don't look at Bubbles and think about how you'd like to stick a fork in her eyeball.

I stopped at their table, my eyes widening when I saw Mila.

"Hey, you," she said in surprise, a big smile on her face.

I filled in the gaps, remembering how she said she was a PR person.

"Your clients?" I asked, indicating Sebastian and Spider, and she nodded. Relief filled me because I liked her. A lot. But if she'd been seeing Sebastian, then I'm not so sure how I would have felt. Not sure why that mattered anyway, since he was obviously seeing Blair.

Spider looked from me to her. "You guys know each other?"

"We bonded over coffee and a mutual distrust of boob jobs," she said on a giggle.

Sebastian crossed his arms, effectively dropping hands with Blair. His eyes darted over my shoulder, and I followed his gaze and found Phil's angry face and the hostess girl's look of rapture.

I sighed. "That's my boss. He didn't want me coming over."

"You didn't mention this is where you worked," he said, a hint of accusation in his voice.

"She did to me," Mila chimed in. "I can't wait to hear her play the violin."

I looked at Sebastian. "You didn't mention you were coming

here on a date," I said.

Blair's eyes were daggers as they raked over me. "Well as you can see, he *is* on a date."

I ignored her and poked Spider in the arm and nodded my head at his drink. "You want me to come over tomorrow and make you another green drink? Don't think I didn't see you pour it out this morning before I left."

He grinned and toasted me with his whiskey glass. "*This* is the best hangover remedy I need, but if you do come, I'll make sure I have my pants on next time." He chuckled. "I just can't promise I'll drink what you make."

An older man sitting with them, who'd been studying me, spoke. "You must be the new neighbor Sebastian mentioned earlier." He shook my hand. "I'm Harry Goldberg, their agent."

"Nice to meet you," I said warily. With stark white hair and beady eyes, he had a sharp look to him, as if there wasn't much he missed.

Blair's face was hard as she looked at me. "Don't you work at the coffee shop in the Grant Plaza? The one with the low-fat Frappuccino's everyone raves about?"

"No," I said.

Her eyes turned into slits. "You sure? I could have sworn I'd seen you there."

I smiled tightly. "I'm pretty sure of where I work. It's here."

I gave Sebastian a searching look. *Why was he with her?*

"No, really, I think I've seen—"

"Can you join us for a few?" Sebastian asked, cutting her off. Here we go. Cold then hot. Up then down.

"I don't want to bother you during your meal, plus I have to go on soon." My hands shook at the thought. I sucked in a breath, trying to chill out.

Concern flickered over his face. "V, sit down. Please."

I touched my cheeks. They felt clammy.

"You are so sweet to worry about some little waitress," Blair cooed as she leaned in and kissed Sebastian lightly on the lips. I watched as Mila clawed at her like a kitten from behind. But I couldn't laugh. I wanted to crawl under the table.

Spider touched my hand, as if sensing my thoughts. "Here, sit by me."

I nodded and settled in next to him. He tossed a tattooed arm around me and gave me a little hug. His other arm was already around Mila. He glanced at us both and grinned. "Bloody hell, I've got two beautiful birds on either side of me. All we need now is a dark room, a big-ass bed, and some lube."

I burst out laughing along with Mila. He was just teasing, of course, but Sebastian's jaw clenched as he stared at us. I let my eyes rove over the rest of him, taking in the tousled hair, the blazing blue eyes, the fullness of his lips—even if they did seem a bit tight. He might be with Blair, but he *was* angry that I was sitting next to Spider. It made no sense.

As Sebastian and Blair ducked their heads to talk to each other, Spider chuckled from beside me and whispered. "Blair's getting her knickers in a wad at the way you're staring at her man."

Shit! I flicked my eyes over at her red face and then turned back to Spider. "Why does she hate me?" I whispered.

Spider cocked an eyebrow at me. "Babe, you're hot. Sebastian's the one who's making it worse. He can't take his eyes off you. He saw you come out from the back with your boss and nearly flipped his lid. I think he thought you were on a date."

With Phil?

"He blew me off last night," I murmured. "I don't think he

really cares."

Spider nodded. "He's had a rough time of it. Putting up with me, managing the band—and now Blair. I don't know how he keeps it together. He's my best mate, and if it wasn't for him, I'd probably be dead. Or back in rehab." He sighed. "We didn't come here just to make movies, you know. Part of the reason he wanted to settle down in LA was to get me off the road for a while. He's a good guy. Always has been."

I nodded.

Harry said something to me and I turned back to face the table. "Sorry. What was that?" I asked.

Harry spoke again, his keen eyes on me. "I asked if you'd ever worked on a set?"

"No." I shook my head, fighting the need to tap. Or squirm. Or something.

"You have an agent?"

"No."

"She used to live in New York," Mila said to him. "She's new here."

His eyes speared me. "Huh. New York? You look like someone I know—"

"Why would she need an agent? She plays classical music in a restaurant," Blair interrupted in a lofty tone. "And not the best one in town either. Really, Harry, what were you thinking in coming here? This place is truly awful."

"Her music isn't classical by any stretch of the imagination," Sebastian said softly, his eyes boring into mine.

Blair stared at Sebastian, her face cold. "There's a weird undercurrent between you two that needs to stop before anyone else notices." She pointed out the window at a group of paparazzi who were standing on the sidewalk waiting for celebrities to walk by. "They don't miss much of anything these days."

I blinked, unsure how to take her comments.

"Wait, I do know you!" Blair exclaimed, turning back to me. I flinched. "You're that girl who ran out of the coffee shop after making a huge mess. No wonder you didn't want to admit you worked there. You're also the girl Sebastian was with at the ice cream shop." She sent Sebastian a scowl. "Did you plan this? Are you trying to ruin our careers?"

What? That was insane. I didn't want to ruin them.

Harry, who'd been sitting quietly, surfing on his phone, snapped his head up, a look of triumph on his face. His voice boomed across the table. "You're Violet St. Lyons, that heiress who was in the plane crash. I *knew* you looked familiar." He proudly showed them his phone, scrolling through pictures of me being hauled up in a rescue helicopter and one of me coming out of the Dublin hospital.

No!

"Who?" Sebastian said, a look of confusion on his face as he studied the phone. I wasn't surprised. It was New Yorkers who knew my face by heart.

Harry added, "You know . . . the plane that was bombed on its way to Dublin? There were articles written about her for weeks. It was her eighteenth birthday, and they found her floating on—"

"Stop," I gasped out, my heart in my throat. I couldn't breathe.

All eyes swiveled to me, and memories hit me.

The explosion.

Bodies being sucked out the hole.

My mother.

My father.

Water.

Darkness.

The panic attack took over, cold chills racing down my spine even as fire blazed over me. Hot. Cold. I clutched the table, lungs burning, black spots dancing in my eyes. My stomach rolled, and it felt like cotton was in my mouth. I swallowed convulsively, keeping down bile.

Please, not here, not in front of Sebastian and his friends— and Blair.

"V?" Sebastian said as he jumped up from his seat and scooted in next to me. He clutched my shoulders. "What's wrong?"

Breathe! It's not that hard!

I practiced my exercises. Inhale . . . exhale.

"She's losing it, mate," Spider said, a worried tone in his voice.

"Talk to me," Sebastian said, trying to lift my chin.

"Need . . . to catch . . . breath." I closed my eyes.

Someone *pff*ed. "You've got to be kidding me. She's obviously faking for attention or she's trashed."

"Shut the fuck up, Blair," Sebastian snarled. "She's freaking out because Harry brought up that plane crash."

"Do we need to call an ambulance?" Mila asked.

"I don't know. Shit. Maybe," Sebastian replied.

I held my hand up. "Done this . . . before. Wait." My chest rose rapidly.

"I'm not waiting. This is crazy, V," Sebastian barked out as his arms swept underneath me. He picked me up from my seat. "I'm getting you out of here."

Everyone in the entire restaurant was probably staring by now. I molded myself to him and hid my face in the hollow of his neck. "Thank you," I whispered.

"Fuck. I'm so sorry," he said, carrying me across the floor.

He was sorry? I was mortified.

I opened my eyes when Phil came up and guided Sebastian back to his office. He left us there as Sebastian carried me inside and positioned me on the couch.

I pressed my face against the cool leather. God. I wanted to crawl inside it and disappear.

"Here, this should help," he said, and placed a bottle of water in my hands. He must have taken it from Phil's desk.

"I'm sorry," I said after a few moments. "Thank you for getting me out of there."

"You have *nothing* to apologize for. Harry—"

"Don't," I said. "What you saw out there, I've done numerous times. It's part of the reason I don't play in public." I rubbed my face.

"I get that." He sat next to me and hugged me tight as if he did it everyday. I didn't protest. He idly doodled on my arm. "What's the other reason you don't play anymore?"

I sighed. "After my parents—it's hard to be the person I used to be."

He gave me a squeeze. "Want to know what happened to me once on stage?"

I gave him a small smile. "I can't see you ever doing anything embarrassing."

He shrugged. "Ha, well, one night we were playing a show in New Orleans at the House of Blues—the biggest one we'd had at that point. I was only twenty and a nervous wreck, so I sucked down some vodka before the show. Then, right in the middle of a song, my drunk ass tripped over some wires on stage and I fell flat on my face. The whole place died laughing." He chuckled. "Busted my lip, chipped a tooth, *and* broke my nose." He pointed to his front tooth where I saw a minuscule line. "Had to get a veneer put on."

I sighed at the image of him on stage. Chipped tooth or not, he'd be beautiful. "My freak-out didn't freak you out?"

He shook his head. "Not at all. Made me want to jump across that table and smack Harry for getting you upset." He searched my eyes. "And, I'm sorry to hear what happened to you. I lost my parents too, so I understand how grief changes a person. I was just a kid when it happened, but the pain that comes with loss doesn't have an expiration date."

His words moved me, but I didn't want to go there. It hurt too much.

I flicked my eyes back up at his face, taking in the softened jawline, the careful way he touched my hand. I snuggled into his side. "You smell amazing," I murmured.

"Yeah, well, you're trying to change the subject, but I'll go with it—because you may not know this, but I love to talk about myself."

"You're a cocky bastard," I said on a laugh.

He inclined his head. "Thank you."

I grinned. "And, I see what you're doing . . . making me laugh when I really just want to hide and never have to face those people again. I'm probably fired, too." I looked down at our now intertwined hands.

"Meh, this place sucks anyway. Plus, I didn't like how your boss looked at you. I say you let me find you a real gig somewhere."

"Really?"

He nodded and we were quiet for a moment until, "So, how *do* I smell?" he asked.

The words tumbled out. "Like the brine from the ocean just as the sun is coming up. Like the softest, most expensive man's shirt I've ever touched. Like the most delicious piece of chocolate I've ever had on my tongue—" I stopped short and buried my face in his shoulder. "Gah, I went too far, didn't I?"

He tipped my chin up. "You sound like you've put some thought into it."

"Maybe."

"So you think about me?" he asked.

I nodded. "Mostly at night when I play . . . and then later when I go to bed. I see your face, and it helps me sleep."

He pushed a stray hair out of my face, his fingers tracing the curve of my cheek. "You're different, V, not like anyone else I've ever met." His voice was husky.

"Different like I might need to check myself into a sanitarium? Different like I might need to use stronger deodorant?"

His gaze captured mine. "Different like I've never met anyone with eyes the color of lavender. Different like hearing you play, *then* seeing you nude was the highlight of my year." He stroked my lips with his fingers. "Different like your mouth is the sexiest thing I've ever seen."

"What about Blair? She isn't your girlfriend?"

He paused, a struggle on his face until he seemed to come to a decision. He exhaled heavily. "It's just pretend for the media so I can get more clout in Hollywood, specifically a Hing move."

"Oh." That was a surprise. "So you *don't* want her?"

"You're the one I want, V. I want to take you to the fucking stars with my mouth. I want to make you come so hard you can't even think of me without wanting my hands on you . . ."

I moaned. He'd escalated fast.

"Exactly," he whispered as his lips took mine. His hands held my face, his fingers splayed out against my cheeks as he explored my mouth with a gentleness that broke me.

But I wanted more. Heat. Sharpness. Roughness.

"Harder," I managed to say when our lips separated.

His chest rose as he stared at me intently. "I didn't bring you back here for this, but if we start, I can't promise I'll stop this time."

"I didn't ask you to stop."

He growled and came back at me. Desperate. Clutching his hair, I gave it back to him tenfold. Our lips were wild, greedy, hands and mouths and teeth demanding payment from the other, as if we'd waited an eternity to find each other.

This is what I'd craved since the moment I'd played for him.

"Can I touch you?" he breathed, his eyes heavy-lidded, imploring me to say yes.

I nodded and unbuttoned my dress until it slipped down my shoulders and drifted to my waist.

"V, you're too much," he hissed and tugged my demi-bra down until my breasts spilled out. He traced light circles around my areolas, making me crazy until finally he fingered my nipples and twisted.

I gasped. "Just like that," I whispered. "Again."

His mouth captured my breast, his tongue lashing at my tender skin, teasing me with flicks and pulls. His teeth nibbled at me, and I arched my back. Closer. *Yes, yes, yes.* I bit his neck, and he dug his fingers into my waist and groaned.

"Yes," I breathed as he shoved my dress down further, his fingers teasing the waistband of my panties.

He pressed his forehead to mine and stared into my eyes. "I've been dreaming of this since you played that first night. I've wanted my cock inside you while you played . . . you on my lap, my hands on your ass, your tits in my face . . . damn, it sounds weird when I say it out loud."

Desire knifed through me. "I like it," I breathed. "Say it again."

"Straddle me first," he said.

I did and he shuddered as I ground myself against his hardness.

He tossed his head back. "V, don't ever stop what you're doing."

I didn't plan on it. My dampened panties slid over his jeans as he massaged my breasts, his fingers plucking my nipples, stretching them out. I arched my back, my body burning to have him inside me. *Yes.*

He tore out of his jacket like a madman, and I helped yank his shirt off, until finally our flesh met skin to skin. His muscled pecs quivered as he clutched my back and held me, his breath coming in gasps.

"You're shaking," I murmured.

"I'm fucking dizzy over you, V." The words came out haltingly as if he didn't understand it.

"Me, too." I unzipped his pants, eased my hand inside and stroked him. Full disclosure: his cock was a monster, at least eight inches and as wide as my wrist.

"Scared?" he teased as I paused to take him in.

I licked my lips. Maybe a little. I didn't know if he'd fit.

"I'll go slow," he promised huskily, cupping my face.

Tapping noises seeped into my consciousness, voices invading our sanctuary.

"*Fuck!*" Sebastian said on a groan as someone called his name and then mine.

Then a softer voice whined. Bubbles.

"V, we have to stop," he said, his voice laced with heavy disappointment. He pressed his lips against my neck, bit me gently and then kissed the spot. "Spider's liable to burst in on us."

"Tell them to go away. I want to put my mouth on you first." I stroked him, my fingertips ghosting over the head and twirling, rubbing the wetness from him down his length.

"V," he ground out, swiveling his hips closer to me as I used both hands to pump him.

More knocks. More yelling from Blair.

"*Dammit!*" He stilled my hands. "Look, we have to stop, okay? Not only are they waiting, but this is your boss's office."

Reality hit. *Fine.* I rubbed my face and pushed down my need for him. Why did I always do the wrong thing when it came to him? First, I'd kissed him, and now I'd practically begged him to fuck me. I sat back. I needed to breathe.

He kissed me gently and stood to tuck his shirt in. "Plus, I need to check on Blair. We're supposed to go to a club tonight for pics." He touched my face. "You wanna come too? Maybe we can sneak—"

"What? Sneak in another office? A bathroom?" I stood as well. Nope. This was all wrong.

"Okay, if that's out, then let's meet back at my place later, then. What do you say?" He cupped my shoulder and tried to pull me to him, but I resisted.

I pulled out of his touch and adjusted my bra, refusing to meet his eyes.

How could he be so cool now?

"I don't think so."

He stiffened at my sharp tone. "Hey, don't be mad at me. I was up front with you about her."

The old me reared up. She'd been doing it more and more

lately, and I was glad to see her. "Yeah? Well, let me be upfront. I don't play second violin. I play first. Always."

He groaned. Exasperated. "Listen to me. I want you in my bed. I'm done trying to stay away from you, V, but we have to make sure the press doesn't know. It would look bad if I was caught 'cheating' on her." He stroked my face, his hands trailing down to my breasts where he thumbed my nipples.

My heart dipped. "Wait. So this is just about sex *and* you want to keep it a secret?"

He shrugged, a wary look growing on his face. "Don't you? You don't seem like the type to like the kind of attention I garner."

"I won't share you with Blair, even if it is pretend." I inhaled a sharp breath. "I've been running from relationships for two years, Sebastian, and I'm ready to stop. I didn't even realize it until now but—I want something more. I'm ready."

He stiffened and took a step back from me. "Don't make me choose between you and her, because she's my career."

"You don't need her to make it big, Sebastian. Make other movies."

"This one will make me a star." He paced around the room. "My brother gave up his music for me. He quit his band and raised me, and I—I want to make him proud, V. I don't expect you to get it. Apparently, you're an heiress."

I threw up my hands. "You live in the Hollywood Hills. Isn't that making it?"

"I want more, V. I always have. Maybe it's because I started with nothing." He rubbed a hand through his hair, straightening it where I'd mussed it.

"Are you sleeping with her?"

He crossed his arms. "This feels like an interrogation. You

don't own me, V."

He didn't answer me. Which meant *yes*.

I wiped at my lips. Trying to scrub him off me.

His chest heaved, an uncertain expression on his face. "Look, I don't want to fight with you. I just want to have fun."

He wanted to get laid.

I gave him nothing but silence as I buttoned my dress.

He sighed. "I'm trying to give you honesty here."

"Well, it hurts," I whispered.

A mask fell over his face, distance building in his eyes as he stared at me. Regret and perhaps even sadness flashed over his face. "Shit. I never want to be part of your pain, V."

More knocks. More whining. This time I twirled around and opened the door.

Spider bounded in with Mila and Blair right behind him.

"Cover your eyes, girls, they're naked," he exclaimed and then laughed at our expressions. "What's up with the weird faces? Wait, were you two shagging? For reals?"

"No," we both snapped.

Sebastian slipped on his jacket and nodded his head toward the door. All businesslike. "What did we miss out there?"

Spider smirked. "Ah. You missed dessert and Blair's scintillating conversation; Harry had to leave, it's past his old-man bedtime; and most everyone in the room took pics of you carrying V around like some kind of modern day Rhett Butler. I predict a full-color spread in the *Hollywood Insider* tomorrow."

Sebastian groaned.

"You and I had a deal, and you're ruining it with this girl," Blair bit out. "No one crosses me, Sebastian."

"Chill out with the drama. I had a panic attack, and he was helping me," I said to her. "That was it."

She gaped at me like I was an idiot. "Reporters spin what they want, and him leaving me for some upstart is huge. Hello, Brad and Jennifer? Demi and Ashton?"

Please. No way was she that big.

Spider swatted her on the butt. "Come on, Blondie, I'm sure there will be more pic opportunities for you and Sebastian later. Let's get you to the club where you can shake that arse."

She sent Spider a cutting look and took Sebastian's arm. "You ready? I'm sick of this place and your friends."

Sebastian exhaled heavily, his eyes on me. Of course, he'd chosen her—we barely knew each other.

He looked at Mila. "You mind making sure V gets home?"

"I drove here. I can drive home," I snapped.

He tried to argue, but I ignored him until he gave up.

They walked out the door. Beautiful stars going out to follow their dreams.

Once, I'd been a star, too, with my music, but I'd allowed the darkness to swallow me up.

Phil swept into the room and tossed my violin case at my feet. "You're fired," he snarled and showed me the door.

I gasped and ran to the case and opened it, running my hands over the strings, checking for injury. I let out a sigh. Thankfully, everything seemed fine.

My heart was another story.

CHAPTER 8

"I'd helped my brother Leo find his one true love, but I'd never told a girl I loved her. Not even Emma."—Sebastian Tate

THAT NIGHT I ARRIVED HOME FROM THE CLUB AROUND TWO. Grouchy and tired, all I wanted was to crash in my bed. But as soon as I walked in the door, I got energized and put Monster on her leash and headed out for a walk.

I was going to V's to check on her. That was all. No kissing. No messing around.

Spider claimed I was *off my trolley* when it came to her, and maybe he was right. Sure, I'd had plenty of pretty girls in my life, but this morning when she shared that she'd lost her parents, my gut recognized there was more than just lust between us. Something deeper connected us, a natural instinct.

I came to a halt at the bottom of her drive. Judging by her dark house, she was already asleep. Disappointed, I paced around on the street, debating if I should wake her. I fingered my phone. I could call her. But what if she was still angry? What if she never played for me again? What is she was still upset from Harry? I wanted to see her; I didn't want to see her. It was fucking ridiculous.

As if Monster knew my thoughts, she tugged me up V's drive. I came to a halt at the big front door and stood there, shifting from one foot to the other.

Just then an overhead light flicked on. *Shit.*

Without thinking too hard about it, I knocked on the door gently. More than likely, the light was from a motion sensor and she was in bed.

I got nothing but silence.

Didn't I deserve it? I'd gone too far with her at the restaurant. Again.

A light in one of the front rooms clicked on. *She was up.*

I knocked harder this time. "V, it's Sebastian. I just wanna talk," I said, resting my hand against the door.

That was a lie. I wanted to do way more than that. I wanted her under me, calling my name while I pounded into her. I wanted her straddling me, riding me—I sucked in a sharp breath.

I pressed my forehead against the door. "I know you're in there. Your lights are on."

Soft footsteps approached the door. "Go away, Sebastian. It—it's late and you shouldn't be here," she said, and I heard the hurt there, in the halting way the words came out.

I stroked my hand across the door. "Let me see you at least before I go."

Nothing.

"Please."

"Where's Blair?" she asked.

"She went home." She'd been trashed and after a lot of coaxing from me, I'd gotten her in a limo and dropped her off. She lived a few streets over so it wasn't uncommon for us to ride together to events where we wanted to be seen together.

"Have you slept with her?"

I closed my eyes and swore under my breath. "One time, before I even moved to LA. It was a hook-up, plain and simple. I haven't touched her since." I paused. "It's crazy, but I haven't been with anyone since I saw you play your violin."

Silence on the other side.

"Look," I sighed. "I've been alone for a long time, and a girlfriend isn't part of my vocabulary, and if you don't want to have a casual relationship with me, I get that, you're at a different place than me. But for whatever it's worth, I'm glad I was there when you had your panic attack, so I could be the one to take care of you—shit, I don't know what all that even means—just let me see your face." I'd had more to drink than I realized. I was rambling all over the place.

She opened the door, and I sucked in a breath at how pretty she looked with her long black hair spilling around her shoulders. Some of it was in her face, and I reached out and tucked it behind her ear.

"Hey, Violin Girl."

"Hey, Blond Guy."

"You look better." I fiddled with my jacket, feeling shy for one of the few times in my life. "I was worried about you."

She stood there, fidgeting in her black dress.

"I didn't wake you?" I asked.

"No, I was up having some tea." Her eyes darted back over her shoulder.

I nodded. "I know this is kinda spur of the moment, but let's get out of town this weekend. Just friends. Spider and Mila, too. We can wear sunglasses and pretend to be tourists, maybe drive to Napa—"

"I can't go anywhere this weekend. Something unexpected has come up."

Disappointment ran over me, but I nodded. I shouldn't have suggested it anyway. "Okay."

We stood there uncomfortably and I touched her forehead. "You've got this little frown right there, and it's killing me to think you're mad at me. Can we move forward, forget about Blair?"

She let out a weighty sigh and flicked a glance over her shoulder. *Again.* "Can we talk tomorrow? I'm busy right now."

At two in the morning?

My gut twisted. "Why? Is someone here?" I cocked my head. Listening.

"No," she said, but her eyes avoided mine.

"No? You're acting weird. You sure you're good? Don't need me to check any closets or look under your bed?" I eyed her foyer but didn't notice anything out of the ordinary.

Rustling came from inside her house, and I snapped, adrenaline driving me as I brushed past her. She shoved back at me, and I stumbled backwards, my hand catching on a porch post.

Her chest rose rapidly. "I don't like this side of you, Sebastian. Now, *please leave.*" Two spots of color blazed on her cheeks.

Fury swarmed in me like angry wasps. Who was she protecting?

"Is Spider in there?" I bit out. He'd suddenly up and left the nightclub we'd been at. I'd tried to call and text him, but he'd never answered. Neither had Mila.

She lifted her chin. "Why? I don't own you and you don't own me. Isn't that right?"

Then I saw it . . .

A set of leather luggage and a pair of men's loafers parked next to a pair of girly heels and a purse.

I paced around her porch, fists clenched. "Who's in there with you, V?"

Just then an auburn-haired dude waltzed up behind her and settled his hands on her shoulders, all easy like. But his gaze was hard as nails as he raked over me and obviously found me lacking if the curl of his lip was anything to go by.

"Violet?" He said her name gently, his voice sandpaper on my brain. His hands smoothed down her arms to lean into her, his nose right in her neck. "You said to hang back, but I'm not so sure, sweetheart." His lips snarled as he considered me. "Your friend giving you trouble?"

I wanted to give *him* trouble. I shoved a hand through my hair, pulling on it at the end, trying to ground myself.

She shook her head, her eyes still on my face. "No, he's fine."

He didn't seem convinced as he eyed me with disdain. I sized him up, too. Wearing dress slacks and a cream-colored fisherman's sweater, he looked like a Ralph Lauren ad. Everything I wasn't. I flexed my biceps, itching to reach in, pluck him out of the house and put my fist in his face.

And it *was* insane. Because she wasn't my girlfriend, yet here I was, losing my shit.

"Geoff?" I bit out.

He nodded, brown eyes burning with a banked anger. "And you must be the infamous rock star next door. I've heard about you." He smirked and glanced at V. She looked back at him, and it was a look I wasn't part of. It said *I know you.*

"Look at *me*, V," I said and she raised her eyes to mine.

"Are you—are you with him?" I asked, part of my brain not wanting to process what was obvious.

She didn't speak.

"It's not a hard question," I muttered.

Geoff crossed his arms. "Explain it to him, Violet," he said, leaning against the jamb of the door.

She licked her lips. "We're friends," she said.

"Who used to be lovers," Geoff said slyly. "In fact, at one

point, she was almost my *wife*."

Coldness hit me at my core, and I had to suck in some air. *She'd been engaged to this uptight asshole?*

"You went from him to me?" I shook my head and barked out a laugh. "Perfect, just perfect. It's like my ex all over again."

V opened her mouth and then closed it, her eyes shifting from me to him. She settled on him. "Geoff, will you give me a minute?"

"Sure. I'll go find us a movie while you take care of *this*." He sent me a smirk. "Call out if you need help." He walked back into her house.

She turned to me. "Sebastian—" she started, but stopped when I shook my head.

"Just stop. Nothing you say will make this better. Maybe I deserve seeing you with him after ditching you for Blair. I know we aren't anything to each other." I exhaled heavily, struggling to let my anger go. "Maybe—maybe I'm just relieved."

"Relieved?"

"You *lied* to me."

"Sebastian, wait—"

"No, you wait. I hate liars," I ground out. "It's why I'm brutally honest. Liars rip your guts out when the truth is always the best damn answer. I gave you truth. I told you what I was about, yet, you—you chose to lie. All you had to say was that your ex was in your house, only you didn't."

"I didn't know he was coming. He just showed up when I got home." She took a step toward me but stopped when I backed off the porch.

"Liars always have good excuses, V."

"You're being unfair." She spread her hands apart. "It's been a year and a half since I've seen him. I had no idea—"

I held my hand up. The television had clicked on from inside the house, a stark reminder that he was waiting for her. I sent her a nod. "Goodbye, V. It sounds like your fiancé is waiting for you. I'll not keep you."

With my chest aching for some unknown fucking reason, I staggered off in the grass between our houses.

&

I woke up to sunlight streaming in my window and a wet kiss.

Monster licked my face, and I groaned. "You need to eat some breath biscuits, baby girl." I flipped over and buried my head under the covers.

"Good morning, Basty," said a cloyingly sweet voice.

What the hell? Foreboding hit. I jerked my eyes open and came face-to-face with Blair Storm, who promptly leaned over and kissed my surprised lips.

I scrambled up off the bed.

Had I? Did we?

I scrubbed my face, racking my brain to piece together what had happened last night. Left V's house in a jealous rage—check. Drank most of a fifth of Jack—check. Stumbled off to bed—check.

So where did she come from?

She propped herself up on her elbows and the sheet fell down to her waist. Her huge tits spilled out, but my cock never even twitched.

"How did you get in here?" I said, whipping around the room. I dressed in jeans and a band shirt.

She threw a pillow at me. "Hey, jerk, you made the booty call, not me."

I did?

My mouth felt like a cotton ball was stuffed in it. I scratched my head. "Hey, um, did we . . . have sex?"

She sighed and laid back down in the bed on her side, posing herself. She draped her hair over one of her melons. "You passed out, I'm sad to say." She sent me a petulant look. "We've had some fun times together. Is it really just pretend for you?"

"Yes. We've had this conversation. This is business, Blair."

"Well, I want more. Seeing you with that horrid girl made me realize something. I have feelings for you. Like serious. My heart actually ached when you took her in your arms and walked away from me."

"Your pride was hurt. You don't really care about me." She was too vain and self-absorbed to care about anyone but herself.

She clutched her throat like I'd hurt her and her eyes watered. "How—how can you say that? *I love you, Sebastian.*"

My mouth gaped. She'd say anything—do anything for her career.

Was I much better?

"You have no idea what love is," I said softly. Love is what Leo and Nora had. Love is what my parents had. Real and true love is what I wanted—someday.

I headed to the bathroom and swallowed down some Tylenol. I stared at my reflection in the mirror. I looked like shit, and my mind automatically went to the reason. What was V doing now? Was she waking up in Geoff's arms this morning? Was he touching her in all the places I'd dreamed about?

Blair padded through the doorway. Nude. "Get dressed, Blair."

She ignored me. "What's for breakfast?"

I splashed cold water on my face. "Uh, we don't really have

anything. I suggest you go home to eat."

"We can go to Java and Me?"

I sighed. *Fuck.*

"You know, maybe I *don't* love you like I said," she admitted as she peered at her reflection and checked the waddle under her neck.

"You don't say."

She shrugged. "But, we could take our relationship further—at least for the press."

I tensed. "How?"

"Like an engagement. Wouldn't it be fun to go ring shopping? Next thing you know everyone will be looking for my baby bump."

She was batshit crazy. "Blair, that's not a good idea right now."

"Why? Because you got the hots for your neighbor?"

"No."

"Can I at least borrow some clothes? Mine are wrinkled," she snapped.

I sighed and tossed her some athletic shorts with a drawstring and a shirt. "Look, I have a massive headache, and all I want to do right now is get some coffee. Why don't you come downstairs when you're done up here and we'll talk."

She sighed. "You may have already ruined your chance for the movie last night. We need to get behind this and make an appearance so everyone sees we're still together."

I groaned. I didn't want to pose for any more fake pictures.

"Don't let your neighbor ruin what you've been working on for weeks," she said as she eased up next to me and slipped her hands inside my jeans to cup me. "You need someone like me. Who wants the same things you do."

"Yeah?" It was hard to think, especially when she fell to her knees, pushed my jeans down and took me in her mouth.

I got hard and closed my eyes, but it was V's face that popped in my head. Fuck. I felt sick. I pulled away from Blair and tucked myself back in. I wasn't going there with her. Not when V was the girl I wanted.

She wiped her mouth and stood, a calculating look in her eyes. "I don't get on my knees for everyone, Sebastian."

I gritted my teeth. "Not in the mood for your drama, so step back."

She relented, pouting. "Fine. You told me last night we'd spend the day together. Are you changing your mind on that too?"

I began to have my doubts and made a note to check my phone to see if I'd even called her in the first place. She was a major manipulator, one of the main reasons I did my best to keep her at arm's length—except for that one time.

But if I wanted that movie . . .

"No engagement rings," I snarled.

She shrugged and gave me a peck on the cheek. "As long as we're together."

Great. This day was going to pass as slow as a kidney stone.

CHAPTER 9

"Like a phoenix, I wanted to be reborn. Forged in fire. Strong."
—from the journal of Violet St. Lyons

THE NEXT DAY, GEOFF AND I HEADED TO A BEAUTY SALON SITUATED near Hollywood and Vine. It was called The Black Swan, and it screamed modern hip. I dug the vibe right away as we walked in, taking in the graffiti-style art and eclectic clientele.

"Don't you think you'd have better luck at a place in Beverly Hills?" Geoff said as we got an eyeful of the statuesque cross-dressing beauty at the sign-in desk.

"This place comes highly recommended by Mila." I nodded my head at one of the clients getting her hair cut. "Cyndi Lauper. See, classy."

He arched a brow. "About as much class as a box of pink Zinfandel." He teased, but I sensed the underlying tension. Things were strained between us, which wasn't surprising considering he'd shown up at my door last night in a taxi and asked to stay the night. Part of me had been glad to see him—surprisingly thrilled—but another side of me wondered why he was here.

Then Sebastian had knocked on my door. He'd acted as if me lying about Geoff had hurt him somehow, yet this morning on my run I'd seen Blair leaving his house. I flinched, remembering how she'd strolled out of his house in what must have been Sebastian's clothes. I'd darted behind a bush and hunkered down, watching as he opened her Porsche's car door for her and then stood there as she drove away. *He was the liar.*

"You okay?" Geoff asked, looking at me as we walked to the sign-in desk. "Your face is green."

"I'm fine," I said. But I wasn't. Part of me was nursing a broken heart, and I didn't even understand it. "Anyway, Mila says this is the place to go when you want something unique."

He grunted. "A venereal disease?"

"Be nice. Sebastian and Spider get their hair done here, too."

He gaped at me. "Are you kidding me? I've read up on these guys. They're your typical bad boy rockers, especially Spider."

I groaned. "Don't believe everything you read, Geoff. I've met them both, and while Spider does have some rough edges, I sense a good guy. Sebastian is incredibly talented. He's made a living out of his music—all without a record label. You have to respect that."

His smile slipped and his eyes narrowed. "You sound like his cheerleader. It's annoying."

"Stop being a jealous jerk. It doesn't suit you." I nodded my head at a Hispanic guy with a Mohawk. "That's Steve, the guy Mila got me an emergency appointment with."

He brushed imaginary lint from his shirt and sent Steve a lofty look. "I'd much rather see you at a luxury spa, preferably in Manhattan." He took my hand. "Come on, there's still time to get out of here. We can get on a plane and be in New York by dinner. I'll even take you to Vesper's—that Thai place you loved? It's still there, just waiting."

A block from my parents' Upper East Side apartment, Vesper's had been my favorite place. We'd met Geoff and his parents there several times over the years.

"First off, I don't fly, and secondly, I have a hair appointment, so shut your fancy face and come with me."

He laughed. "Okay."

The receptionist led me over to Steve, who looked ominous with his six-inch Mohawk and ear gauges. Tattoos of skulls were splattered up his muscled arms.

I sat down in the chair, met Steve, and we talked about my hair. He snapped his fingers and two young girls scurried to stand on either side of him. "Ladies, this is V, a friend of the Vital Rejects. She wants a complete reboot. What do you think?"

Their eyes brightened.

"Ah, sexy Spiderman with the blue hair . . ."

". . . black widow, come bite me . . ."

". . . pierced his nipple once . . ."

I cocked an eyebrow at their excitement. "I take it they're good customers?"

They'd continued.

"And Sebastian . . . dirty talking boy . . ."

". . . god of thunder . . . be my hammer . . ."

". . . best hair in town . . ."

I laughed as Steve hushed the girls, who erupted into giggles and left—something about getting foils and color.

"They're a bunch of sluts." He grinned good-naturedly. "You with either of those dudes? I promise it's all in good fun."

Geoff had stiffened at his question as he flipped through a magazine in a seat a few feet away. It was obvious from how territorial he'd acted last night and from the flowers he'd sent me—he wanted another try with me.

The receptionist came back and poured us two glasses of champagne and set them on a small table next to my chair.

"Let's make a toast," I said to Geoff as Steve went to the back to check on the color girls.

He set down his magazine and strolled over. I took him in, my eyes lingering on his designer jeans and golf shirt. He'd bulked up in the past two years, and it didn't go unnoticed. His brown eyes glittered at my attention. I blushed. Caught.

"What are we toasting to?" he asked as he handed me a glass. I inhaled his aftershave, a spicy blend I'd bought for him on special occasions. I felt flattered he still wore it.

I nibbled on my lip. "I don't know. Hope? Love? A good haircut?"

He took my glass from me and set it down. "Forget the toast. Let's talk."

I nodded. Steve was still in the back.

He sighed. "First off, I would have come out here sooner, but you weren't ready. I gave you time, and as soon as I finished undergrad this past semester, the only thing I could think of was seeing you."

I recalled the socialites. "I've noticed you haven't been lonely."

He shrugged. "I'm no monk. And judging by the sexual tension between you and rocker boy, you're no nun."

"I haven't slept with him—but I wanted to."

Pain flashed across his face, but he seemed to readjust as he leaned down and touched my cheek. "You left me eighteen months ago because you needed more time to grieve. I rushed you—I see that now. You packed your bags and walked out of my life, but I've never forgotten you." He took in a quick breath. "I—I want you back."

"You want the old me back." I couldn't be the person he wanted.

"Let me get to know the new you," he said softly, and kissed me on the lips. With gentleness, his lips parted mine, his tongue tasting me. The kiss took me by surprise, yet I fell into it and kissed him back, part of me yearning for my past and someone who had loved me—*still loved me?*

"At least that part of us hasn't changed," he whispered against my lips.

"I'm a college drop-out with a tapping problem," I murmured.

"You can still go back."

"You think the Manhattan School of Music would have me?"

A fire lit in his eyes. "I'll hand in the application myself. Better yet, I'll call up the chancellor and request a meeting. You were a prodigy, Violet. They'd be nuts to not let you in."

I tried to picture me sitting in a classroom now. It seemed far-fetched, plus I'd burned bridges when I left. Friends I hadn't called back. Professors I'd ignored.

"Come back to New York," he implored.

I sighed. "I have the orphanage to think of. I haven't been as active as I should have, but that's going to change. I have a gala to plan."

He grabbed my hand. "Open another one in New York."

Perhaps.

But something—or someone—was holding me back.

And then there were all the memories.

My stomach knotted, and I closed my eyes briefly and then met his intense ones. "Geoff, my last night in New York, I stood on the ledge of my apartment building for two hours in the freezing cold debating if I was going to jump or not."

His eyes flared. "God, I'm sorry. Why didn't you ever tell me?"

I stared at my hands. "You didn't want to know how far I'd cracked. You say you want to get to know me, but the thing is, you may not like the darkness."

Emotion worked his face. "You're my heart, Violet, since the moment I saw you. I can't give up on you."

And me? I still loved him—in the way you'd love an old movie or a favorite quilt.

Needing a topic change, I picked up our glasses and handed him his. "My parents named me after a comet, so let's toast to that—to stepping out of the shadows and shining bright."

"I say we throw a toast to us in there as well. To new beginnings."

I inhaled sharply at his words, at the heaviness of them. Sebastian had liked new beginnings too.

Not knowing what to say, I held my glass up and we clinked them together.

CHAPTER 10

"My heart is a reckless thing, willing to say or do anything to get the reaction it wants."—Sebastian Tate

SITTING INSIDE JAVA AND ME, I STARED DOWN AT THE PHOTOS ON my phone. A tingle of foreboding went up my spine.

Out of all the pic ops I'd posed for last night with Blair, the *Hollywood Insider* had run with three pictures I'd never posed for as the top story on their website. No doubt it would make their television show this evening.

The first was of me carrying V through Masquerade. The second was a fuzzier pic of us kissing in the manager's office, obviously taken from the window outside the restaurant. *Fucking reporters.* And finally, the last photo was of me and Blair arguing outside the club when I'd told her I was taking her home.

Mystery Girl and Sebastian Tate was the tagline.

Disaster. All that time invested with Blair, and it had fallen apart in one day.

"I hate to say it, but Blair was right." I inspected the pic of us in the office. I squinted as I turned the photo in different angles. "That could be anyone. Right?" I looked to Mila for help.

She leaned over my shoulder and patted my arm—not a good sign. "Hmmm, I can tell that's your hands on V's butt by your lion ring, and that's definitely your big old head and blond hair." She giggled. "What cracks me up is the little black-out line where V's boob is."

She pointed at the one of me carrying V after her attack. "What I find interesting is the way you look here. All Neanderthal like, 'Me caveman. Me protect my woman,'" she joked in a deep voice.

I arched a brow. "Glad you're amused. You're not much help."

Spider smirked at me as he sipped on his tea. "These pics explain why Blair ran out this morning—thank God." He shuddered.

I nodded. She'd left as soon as her PR girl had gotten a tip from someone who worked at the *Hollywood Insider*.

Mila patted my hand. "Just read what it says out loud. Maybe we can spin it." She tried to sound chipper, but I had a feeling that once Hing saw that I wasn't with Blair anymore—that we were arguing—he'd think twice about hiring me.

"You just want to make fun of me," I said as I scrolled down on my phone to get to the article.

"No, I want to help."

"I want to make fun of you," Spider snarked.

I flipped him off and read the article.

"Is there a new leading lady in Sebastian Tate's life? Rumors are he and girlfriend Blair Storm are in bad weather. How does this *Hollywood Insider* know? Because the Vital Rejects' front man was photographed kissing a mystery girl while at a restaurant in Beverly Hills last night. Onlookers reported he swept her up in his arms and escaped to a back room with her after an altercation with his girlfriend, actress Blair Storm, 33. Tate, 23, shared more than just handholding with the brunette beauty while in the back room. The employees of the restaurant claim the new gal pal is a violinist

who works for the restaurant, although sources have not been confirmed. Others claim Sebastian and Blair headed to a club later, but that things between them seemed strained. Is there trouble in paradise between these two stars who have reportedly been dating since April? Who is this mystery lady and will we see her again? Has Tate decided that Blair Storm is too old to weather? Our reporters will keep you up to date as this story develops. Text our tip line with your news and stories."

Spider whistled. "Blair's going to piss herself when she sees this."

As if on cue, my phone ran. *Harry.* The article had been online for ten minutes and he was already calling.

"Asshole agent?" Spider asked

Mila shushed him as I answered.

I opened with, "Harry, it's not a big deal."

"No, it's a fucking disaster when you cheat on America's Sweetheart! Directors don't want relationship issues on their set, Sebastian!" He breathed heavily into the phone. I pictured him sitting at his desk in Beverly Hills, clutching the phone like a lifeline as he visualized millions in a movie deal flying out the window.

I kept my voice soft, but my own anger was building. "This article is bogus. There's nothing between me and V. We're friends."

Were we even that now?

He cackled. "Yeah, right. You screwed up when you kissed her, Tate. While she was topless. Pictures don't lie."

"Fine. How can we fix it?" I snapped.

Silence for a few beats. "Just be seen with Blair, act like

nothing's wrong. At the end of the day, Hing liked your screen test, he digs your look, but he was waffling based on your rep, so I don't know what he's going to do when he gets wind of this."

I sat up straighter. "Harry, to be honest, I'm sick of Blair. She acts like we're really dating and says mean shit to my friends. I don't trust her."

I heard him groan. "Look, I've read the script. *This movie will make you a star.*"

Something V had said came back to me. About how I could make it on my own.

"Maybe I don't need Blair. Maybe there's another movie out there for me."

He sighed. "I've got nothing on my plate for you now. This is it. Sure, you can take a break from Blair and see what happens. But fans are fickle and so are movie studios. By the time a new script comes along, you could be old news."

I fumed. "I still have music, Harry. You're the one who's supposed to get the movie deals. Do your fucking job."

"I'm just saying the truth. Not that I like it." He paused. "Just stay away from that girl, Sebastian. She's career suicide."

I hung up and slammed the phone down. Even though I'd left her house angry, I didn't want to hear I was supposed to stay away from V.

"Holy Hannah in a hand basket, V just walked in the door," Mila exclaimed as she looked over my shoulder.

She was here?

"Where?" I said, heart thundering as I craned my neck around to the entrance.

She whistled. "She's got a sizzling new hair style—and a hottie with her."

"Who you calling a hottie?" Spider snipped.

I narrowed my eyes. Since when did Spider get jealous over guys Mila checked out? He and I were due another conversation.

When I saw her, my mouth dried. Her long hair had been cut to shoulder-length in a choppy style where the front was longer than the back. The ends had been dipped in an electric purple color. It suited her angular face, the softness of her red mouth.

"She looks like a rocker," I murmured.

She ducked her head at the stir of attention she and Geoff caused at the door, the locals wondering if someone important had come in, the tourists checking to see if she was somebody. A couple of people whispered, and I got paranoid they'd connect her with the Mystery Girl in the paper.

I let out a sigh of relief when no one rushed her. Maybe the hair saved her. I remembered that her face had been hidden in most of them too.

Mila stood up from our booth and waved them over.

Great. How the hell was I supposed to deal with her and Geoff in my face?

As they made their way over, Mila sent me a pointed look. "While you were sleeping in this morning with Little Miss Sunshine, I did my research on V. The guy she's with is the Mayor of New York's son. He's in law school, plays polo, and dates socialites."

She patted my hand. Like I was sad or something. Whatever.

"Go on. Finish it. If I know you, you researched the shit out of it."

She nodded. "Her parents were wealthy philanthropists. Apparently, their name is like gold in New York; everyone loved them and they were a pretty big deal in the social scene. After the crash, she had quite a bit of notoriety going on for a while, lots of papers wanting her story."

Mila straightened her headband and sent a look over my shoulder. "Here they come. Act nice because I happen to like her a lot."

Nice wasn't happening. I could tell by the way my leg was bouncing under the table. I was still angry—or hurt—or *something*.

V slid in next to me while Geoff pulled up a chair at the end of the table. The waitress brought us refills and they chatted. I sat back with my leg deliberately pressed against V's, heat firing off in my body at the proximity of her skin.

Mila and Geoff seemed to hit it off right away—birds of a feather—and got into a discussion about mutual society people they knew in Dallas. Spider zoned out by checking his phone, a petulant look on his face as he watched Mila and Geoff's heads together.

V and I just sat there.

Next to each other.

Neither of us looking at the other.

Both of us on a razor's edge.

I looked at Geoff. He wore jeans but still managed to look like a Wall Street man with his short hair and a thick sweater across his shoulders. Didn't he know it was June in LA? Then I saw the smudge of lipstick on his lips, a trace of pink, and my gut clenched. They'd been kissing.

My phone buzzed and I checked it, hoping it was Harry with good news.

It wasn't.

Violet: **About last night, I'm sorry I lied. Truth is, I was surprised to see you. I didn't know what to say.**

I tapped out my reply: **Meet me in the bathroom. I'll tell you what I really think and then you can make it up to me.**

I looked up as I sent it.

She read my text, her fingers over her phone, the pulse in her neck kicking up.

I sent another: **Did you like it when we made out at Masquerade? You know, I can do a whole lot better with more space, more time, and less of your pansy boyfriend.**

She tapped out: **Go fuck yourself.**

She was angry too, and part of me got turned on. Here's the weird part—I'd been an easy going guy most of my life, but with her, I didn't even recognize who I'd become. Combustible and wired to the teeth, our connection was like a bomb about to explode. She was a grenade, and I wanted to pull her pin so bad I could taste it.

Fucking would be better with you, I sent back.

I waited for a reply but nothing came, so I glanced up to see Geoff playing with V's hair, his fingers idly twisting the strands. My eyes flared, my chest heaved, and I cracked. It became crystal clear—he'd come here to get her back.

And I didn't want to let her go.

I tore my eyes off of them and wrote to her: **Did you fuck him?** My heart pounded as I hit send. Please say no.

She replied: **I saw Blair leaving your house this morning. Nice little walk of shame there. Or maybe, I should call it her "I Got Laid Parade."**

Dammit!

I tapped out: **Truth: she came over. Truth: nothing happened. It was YOU I wanted.**

She wrote: **If it was ME you wanted, then why did you leave Masquerade with her?**

I replied: **What else do you want? Blood? Pictures of us are already splattered all over the internet.**

She immediately set down her phone, a worried frown on her face.

Geoff had been talking to Mila, but stopped. "You okay, Violet?"

She looked at me. "How bad is it?"

"What's going on?" Geoff asked us, eyes darting from me to her.

Every ounce of my anger vanished. It had never been about her specifically anyway. "It's just some photos. I've got it covered. Please, don't worry, V. I'll make sure they don't bother you."

She gripped the menu. "Okay."

"Did you want to order something to eat, Violet?" Geoff asked, putting his hand on her arm.

I sucked in a breath. "Why don't you call her V like everyone else?" I ground out.

"Her name is Violet." He tapped his spoon on his coffee cup.

I crossed my arms. "I call her V or Violin Girl, but then was when I was just watching her through my binoculars."

Even Spider, whom nothing fazed, tensed as he adjusted his muffin in different angles and sent me hard looks. I got his message. *Chill out.*

But I couldn't. I wanted to pound on Geoff.

"Her name is Violet St. Lyons, and her family name goes back to the Mayflower, if you care," he told me, studying his fingernails like I was beneath him. "I don't think the police will take kindly to you spying on her, either."

All eyes swiveled to me.

"She could have called the cops. She *likes* me looking at her."

He snorted. "Please. I doubt that. She's classier than that."

"Me watching her *is* our thing, but I'll spare you the details."

I glared at the lipstick on his mouth.

One corner of his lip quirked. "You remind me of a kid who lost his sucker and cries about it, Mr. Tate. I'm sorry you showed up last night and got your eyes opened."

V let out a gasp. "Geoff, stop. There's nothing going on—"

"She's mine," I growled at him. Mila was right. I *was* a Neanderthal. And I fucking embraced it.

"She's been in my bed. Has she been in yours?" He smiled.

I reared back, almost as if he'd slapped me and I'd taken a stumble.

"Geoff! This is ridiculous. You're both acting like children," V hissed.

But all I could focus on was Geoff.

I forced my tense shoulders in a nonchalant shrug and smiled tightly, my hands clenched under the table. "She may not have been in my bed, but she's an incredible musician, Geoff. But the best thing is when she plays nude just for me. Her music is superb, but put it with her hot body and the way she moves—" I groaned and bit my lower lip "—it takes me to heaven, man."

Dead silence and then, "*She plays naked?*" Spider hissed and elbowed me.

V jerked up out of her chair and gave me a disbelieving headshake. Her face had flushed a deep scarlet.

I flinched at the betrayal in her eyes. "Wait." I stood as well, not caring that we had the attention of half the coffee place. "V—shit—that was low. I wanted him to know how things are between us . . ." I came to an abrupt halt when she turned her face away. I'd sounded needy and insecure anyway. *What was she doing to me?*

"You're an asshole," Geoff murmured, shaking his head at me as he put his arms around V.

121

Surprising me, Spider jumped up, his chair making a horrible scooting noise on the tile. He pointed at Geoff. "Bugger me, *you're* the dodgy one. I've been sitting here trying to keep it in, but you'll not be a dick to my mate. Now, get the fuck out of my coffee shop before I bust your face."

A hush settled around us as camera phones popped out.

"Fine by me," Geoff said. He took Violet's hand and led her away.

"That went well," I muttered as I sat back down and scrubbed my face. Dazed.

Spider smoothed down his blue shirt and took his seat, looking surprisingly unruffled. He nibbled on a scone. "I don't know about her, but you're in trouble for holding out on me. *Really?* How could you not let me look when she stripped?"

Mila slapped his hand. "Be quiet. Can't you see he's upset?"

He pouted. "But it was naughty bits. I love naughty bits."

She sighed. "Good grief, I'll show you my tits later."

It barely registered that Mila had said *tits.*

Because I wasn't paying attention, too busy getting a read on Geoff as he followed behind V. I didn't miss the triumphant smirk he shot me as they'd walked away

Geoff: 2. Sebastian: 0.

CHAPTER 11

"He played me like a symphony."
—from the journal of Violet St. Lyons

THE CONFRONTATION AT THE COFFEE SHOP RUINED THE REST OF
Geoff's visit.

I was angry that Geoff had acted like he owned me,
even insinuating that we'd slept together recently. He fumed that
I'd let Sebastian hear me play, when that had been one of the
first things he asked for when he'd arrived at my house. And the
whole naked thing drove him insane.

The one thing we did agree on was to allow him to speak
with the chancellor at the Manhattan School of Music. Maybe it
would spur me on to do *something* with my career.

The next day, I drove him to the airport and walked him to
the security checkpoint. Most of the time I avoided anything that
might trigger memories of the crash, so this was the first time
I'd been inside an airport since that day. I took it in and didn't get
the cold sweats or want to puke. I felt okay—not great—but I
could function.

"You good?" he asked, as we walked past several pilots and
flight attendants.

I nodded. "I know it seems small, but standing here is big."

"I'm glad." He set his bags down and tugged my hand until
our chests were touching. He looked sad, and part of me—the
old me—wanted to make him happy again. I reached up and

kissed him hungrily. Desperately. Trying to find a spark. He groaned and gathered me close.

But it felt wrong.

He sighed heavily as we pulled apart. "You're thinking about *him*, aren't you?"

No. Yes.

I nodded.

He grimaced. "Why him? He's not anything like what I pictured you with."

I shook my head. "Sometimes there isn't an answer—just a feeling." I pushed a strand of auburn hair off his face and cupped his cheek. "Not that it matters because I can see you're still jealous, but I'm *not* with him."

"I think your heart is," he said tersely as regret flickered over his face. "I know I've dated girls after you, but you were always the goal, and somehow, you've already forgotten all about me." He sighed. "I came here for a reason and my offer still stands. If you come back to New York, I'll be the best damn man for you. I *will* make you forget about him."

I smiled. "You make me breathless with statements like that."

He smirked. "But is it enough for you to let this place go?"

"I don't know." There *were* things I missed about New York: the zoo, the pizza, the winter weather. But here I'd played my violin at the base of the Santa Monica Mountains. Here I was growing. Changing.

He fumbled around in his pockets and pulled out my promise ring. It glittered under the lights in the airport. "Whatever happens in the next few weeks, just remember that I still love you, and if you still want this ring, it's burning a hole in my pocket." He paused. "I've carried it with me for a year and a half, Violet. Waiting."

His poignant words tugged at me. Was there a chance for us? Could he love the new me?

My throat clogged and I couldn't speak. I nodded and hugged him.

"I'll call you," he said, and sent me one last lingering look and joined the security line.

I stood and watched until he disappeared into the crowd.

ഇ

That night I crawled into bed with some old photo albums. I flipped through the pictures, looking at the moments captured there. I stroked the lines of my mother's face. I traced my father's smile. I wept. Yes, grief was its own fucking species, and I was tired of breathing it. Living it.

Meeting Sebastian and seeing Geoff again . . . it made me realize that I wanted my world back. And for the first time since the crash, something in me shifted—a desire to just be still and listen to my heart. To my parents.

My father had saved me. Was I going to let it all be for nothing? Is this the life my mother would have wanted for me? To wallow in guilt and sorrow? To give up my dreams?

Adrenaline rushed over me, and my head roared. I clung to it, jumped up and grabbed my violin and ran out to my balcony, too fired up to make it to the patio. I put my bow to the strings and ripped into the opening bars of Fall Out Boys' "The Phoenix". I surrendered myself to the heavy beat, letting the music take me out of myself and back into the girl I used to be. Feeling wild and light-headed, I stripped the song down, turning the low notes into maddening and powerful high notes. I twisted it around and made it mine.

I played furiously, letting all the pent-up anguish out, showing my parents that I still had it what it took to be a star.

I didn't play for grief or loss or even for Sebastian. I played for *Violet*. Me.

And it was good. Euphoric.

The next morning, I drove to Lyons Place and parked in the front. I got out of my car and went inside on unsteady legs. Mrs. Smythe, a longtime friend of my parents, met me at the door and shook my hand. She'd been the perfect choice to oversee the everyday operations of the hundred-bed facility, and I was glad I'd chosen her.

She gazed at me and patted my hand. "Are you ready? If you are, they're all waiting for you in the cafeteria."

I nodded and followed her, muscles rigid, a cold sweat popping out on my skin.

"What do I say?" I gasped out, barely able to talk as we approached a door where I could already hear the low rumble of kids' voices behind it. My heart was banging in my chest and my tapping was out of control.

"Tell them your story, Violet, or don't. They pass no judgment. They've all got their own demons, and knowing that you've been through the same things they have—it means something."

I lifted my violin from its case. Stroked the soft wood. "May I—may I play for them?"

"Of course, my dear," she said.

And so, I walked into the cafeteria that I'd helped design. On the back wall was a mural of the lion at Central Park, his big slumbering eyes golden and full of mystery as a comet zoomed overhead. On the right side was a portrait of my parents. Not a formal one where you'd sit down in front of a photographer, but a casual shot of my dad messing around with his guitar, and my mom gazing at him adoringly. And there I was—sitting on a chair watching them, wearing the soft smile of a girl with fairy dust in her heart.

It was a moment of frozen happiness.

I took a giant breath and looked into the eyes of the kids who waited for me. They stared and I stared back, fighting the panic, and for the first time . . . *winning*.

In a low, halting voice I talked about my parents.

"My father only had one goal in life and that was to make my mother happy. *She* was only happy when she was helping others. They took me to Africa, the Ukraine, even China . . . and through all of our adventures, the lesson they taught me was simple: I was an extremely lucky girl, *but* I was not the only person in the world, and that we only truly know ourselves when we give back. When they died, I—I forgot that for a while. Their legacy and that lesson is why I'm here today. For two years it was the one reason I never could take my own life." I inhaled. "So today, I'm here to commit myself to Lyons Place and make it a home worthy of you."

Silence followed my speech.

And then, among the artifacts of my past, I lifted my violin and played for them.

CHAPTER 12

"Sometimes reaching your dreams isn't all you'd thought it would be."
—Sebastian Tate

"**P**UT YOUR FINGERS HERE FOR THE C NOTE," I INSTRUCTED Kevin, one of the students at Lyons Place as we sat in the music room. About six other students sat around in a circle, all of them here for their second guitar lesson.

I glanced over at Spider, who was helping another group of wide-eyed students in another part of the room. Truth be told, the brass son of a bitch looked quite at home as he pranced around in his blue ensemble, explaining how to hold your instrument.

When I'd come home from my initial visit with Mrs. Smythe and had told him about the place, he'd been surprisingly enthused. Of course, I'd given him a pep talk this morning about his language and behavior before we'd arrived. So far, he'd been clean and chipper. Thank goodness, Mrs. Smythe had been on board with him too. Turns out her husband was English, so she'd been quite taken with him.

Kevin adjusted the guitar and strummed out a basic chord. The music reverberated through the room and I grinned. "Not bad," I said and showed him the next one by placing his fingers where they were supposed to be. "We'll have you playing like Stevie Ray Vaughan before you know it."

He turned red, and I clapped him on the shoulders. "What's

wrong, man?"

"You-you-you're actually teaching me to pl-play the guitar," he stuttered. "It's the coolest th-thing ever."

I smiled, careful to not interrupt his stumbling words. Mrs. Smythe had given me the low-down on how to handle his speech impediment last week as well as explaining how he'd lost his mom in a house fire years before. He was ten years old with fuzzy red hair and a big hopeful smile. His enthusiasm was infectious.

"You're a natural, Kev."

He straightened his shoulders at my praise. "I-I really want to si-sing," he pushed out. "Be fa-famous like you. When I sing, I don't stu-stutter. Gi-girls will like me then."

I squeezed his shoulder. Dude. Been there.

"We can do that, no problem. Chicks dig guys who sing, but being famous isn't all it's cracked up to be, ya know? It comes with a downside too. Sometimes just being yourself is all it takes to get the girl." I tossed him a grin and flipped through some of the music I'd brought along with me.

"Do y-you have a gi-girlfriend?"

My mind went straight to V, and I blinked, feeling that familiar pang I got when I thought of her. I hadn't seen her since the coffee shop two weeks prior. I watched her house each night, of course, scouring her property to look for any sign of her, but she hadn't been playing outside except for once, nor had she been dropping by to make us green drinks. Her car was often gone from her circle drive, too, and it was killing me wondering where she was. Mila assured me she hadn't left for New York with Geoff. I was glad for that at least.

I just missed her.

"Do *I* have a girlfriend?" I mused. "Hmmm, that's a good

question. Apparently, there's a ton of reporters wondering the same thing. You don't work for TMZ, do you?"

He scratched his head. "Don't watch that sh-show."

I chuckled. I liked Kevin more and more.

Of course, there was Blair. Everything in me rebelled at posing for more fake relationship pictures, but I had allowed Mila to release a press statement saying we were still an item. It was a compromise of sorts. Reporters were following us around separately, wondering what was going on, but so far we'd been tight-lipped on the entire thing. Obviously, she still wanted to cling to me because of my younger age, and I still wasn't ready to give up on Hing and the zombie movie. But I wasn't with her in public anymore. She wasn't happy about it.

I glanced back up at Kevin. "I got all sorts of music here. What do you want to do next?"

"G-got any Nirvana?" He sent me a hopeful look.

Hell yeah.

I gave him a fist bump. "Keep that kind of music in your heart, my man, and you'll be playing on the stage with me someday."

His face shone.

A flash of purple hair went by the room and caught my attention.

"Wh-where you going?" Kevin called as I took off for the door at a slow jog.

"Thought I saw someone," I called back. I reached the wooden door, which was much like a classroom door with a thin glass panel above the doorknob. I flung it open and stepped out in the hallway. There was no one there, and I exhaled and paced around. Not only was I dreaming about her, but I was seeing her in places where she clearly wasn't.

I went back in to Kevin.

"Y-you okay?" he asked.

I thought about it. I took in Kevin, seeing how everything I said or did would make an impression. I pushed my melancholy behind me and instead thought of V and how she played like every note was a physical touch. "Music makes everything better, Kevin. Never forget that."

Spider and I left soon after. We walked out to my Hummer and climbed in. Before I started the car, I paused, needing to share. "Teaching those kids—shit, man—that made me feel good. It's like they're teaching me something."

He sent me a long look and I could see from his face that he too had felt it. "Yeah."

I cocked an eye. "Better than the *The Vampire Dairies*?"

He snorted. "Don't get ahead of yourself, mate. Nothing beats The CW."

☙

The next day, V opened her door at seven on the dot ready to run, her hair scraped back in a high ponytail.

And I was waiting. Patiently doing leg muscle stretches on her driveway.

She came to a halt, her eyes big as she took in my running shorts and Vital Rejects T-shirt. "What are you doing here?"

Good question. "I'm sick of not seeing you."

She stood there, a wary expression on her face. It made me ache to soothe her.

I clenched my fists. "I know you're still mad at me, because I never hear you play anymore, and I'm sorry for it. It kills me to think I hurt you. I was a total douchebag to you at the coffee

131

shop when I told everyone you played naked for me. I was a callous dickhead at Masquerade when I just assumed you wanted to have sex with me. I've been full of shit, and I don't deserve to have a girl like you give me a second chance, but I'm asking. Right here. Right now. You are a hundred times better than me. You're beautiful and your music makes me fucking happy, and all I did was make an ass of myself. And if you want Geoff—pompous nitwit, sorry—I'll try hard to be good around him. For some reason that I can't explain, I need you, V." I paused and took in some air. "Will you—will you be my friend? I hope so, because I need to bitch about Spider and Mila—who are probably having sex. Not to mention, Harry called today and told me that Hing is vetting new guys for the role I wanted."

She still stood there. She swallowed.

"Do you want me to go?" I asked.

Had I gone too far with the nitwit remark?

A car went by. A bird called out.

Finally, after what seemed like forever, she spoke. "Douchebag, dickhead, and an ass? Wow, you didn't hold back. I'm impressed." She gave me a grin.

Right then a fluttering took up in my gut. Like butterflies. I didn't try to analyze it or dissect it. I just sucked in a sharp breath and went with it. "Do you forgive me?"

She nodded.

I relaxed, letting go of some of the tension that had ridden me for two weeks.

She frowned. "I'm sad for you about the movie, though. If you hadn't helped me—"

"No, V, stop. Please don't feel guilty for that. I wanted to help you. It's done and over and I'm moving on from it."

She cocked her head. "You'd take it if Hing offered,

though, right?"

"Yeah." I shrugged. "I've been chasing this film for three months—ever since Harry approached me with it before I moved here."

She smiled. "Spider and Mila, huh? The girl who wears pink and the boy with blue hair?" She snickered. "God, it's too much. Can I say anything? Can we tease them?"

I snorted. "If I catch them together, he *will* marry her."

She laughed. "You really do try to be a hero. You try to hide it, but I see it in you."

I tingled all over. "I'm no hero."

But her thinking I was? Shit, that made me giddy.

"You ready to go?" I asked, checking my watch after we'd talked some more, catching up.

She grinned. "You're really going to go on my run with me?"

I flexed a bicep. "Sweetheart, I'm one lean, mean, running machine. I can outrun a gazelle. I can outrun a Bengal tiger. I can run circles around—hey where are you going?"

She tossed a sassy look back at me as she trotted off down the drive. "I'm doing eight miles today. Try not to poke—or puke."

Eight? "You training for a marathon?"

"Just keeping the cheese puffs and tequila at bay. You scared?"

I puffed up and ran with exaggerated motions, high-stepping by bringing my knees up to my elbows. Just to make her smile.

She gasped out a laugh. "Alright, stop before you hurt yourself—or someone sees you."

We ran together that morning, side-by-side, neither of us speaking—just together.

Were we friends? Were we more?

In the end, I decided it was just running.

CHAPTER 13

"Loving means losing."—from the journal of Violet St. Lyons

A WEEK AFTER SEBASTIAN AND I MADE UP, I GOT EXCITED WHEN Mila suggested we get out of town on an overnight camping and horseback riding trip with the boys. Sebastian and I had spent almost every day together since our run, but it was either at his house or mine. Reporters were constantly driving by now—wanting to catch a glimpse of Blair or the Mystery Girl. So far no one knew it was me, and I wanted to stay under the radar.

We all piled in the Hummer and drove up to the canyon and rented horses. Ten minutes into the ride, Mila and Spider, who seemed to have a knack for disappearing together, took off ahead of us on their horses.

Sebastian pulled up next to the slow mare I'd ended up with. "Living on the edge there, V. You better slow your roll or you'll break that pretty neck." He tugged on my ponytail.

I sent an envious look at his stallion. "Coming from the guy who's riding Black Beauty. Why did you have to pick out the pokey one for me? Turtle here is ready for the glue factory."

"Just want you to be safe," he said, and sent me a lingering look, his eyes pausing longer than necessary on the neck of my blouse. Slightly sheer and low-cut, I'd pulled it out of my closet this morning and shouted with glee. Behold, I did have some sexy clothes. True, it wasn't practical for a camping trip, but I didn't seem to care.

He adjusted himself in his saddle and I let my own eyes linger. With his low-slung designer jeans and form-fitting shirt that showed off his toned muscles and tan, he epitomized virility. And sex. My mouth actually watered. We'd been keeping each other at arm's length and so far it was working. Although last night when we'd snuggled on the couch and watched TV, he'd been especially tense. I wasn't stupid. He wanted me, but he didn't want to hurt me either.

He cleared his throat. "If your horse is that slow, you're welcome to ride with me. You can sit up front, and we'll go as fast as you can handle it."

Perfectly innocent words, but my mind went fuzzy with heat.

"Sit in front of you on a horse? In a rocking motion?" I shook my head. "Like that's a good idea."

"You'd like it," he said huskily. "I promise to keep my hands to myself unless you want me to hold you—so you don't slide off."

And so. I pictured me riding in the same saddle with him. Heat pooled in my core and my body twitched. To fight it off, I pulled out a handful of Oreos from my jacket pocket and crammed one in my mouth.

Stress eating? Sexual frustration? Yes. I dreamed about him constantly. I wanted him so badly my lady parts were crying. Yet it wasn't always just about sex. Most times, it was just an image of us together. Holding each other face-to-face.

"What's making your face so red, V?"

An Oreo piece got stuck, and I coughed.

"You okay?" he said with concern and pulled on my reins, making my horse stop.

I swallowed down the piece and rasped out, "Yeah."

He immediately handed me over some water and I chugged it down, but then I realized how manly he smelled with his natural scent and sweat mixed together. A knot formed in my belly. Maybe this trip had been too soon. He was entirely too beautiful.

"What are you thinking?" he said softly.

"The scenery? Uh, it's quite pretty here." I stared into his eyes.

"You're not even looking at the scenery."

I came to and glanced around at the trees and rocks and stuff. "Better?"

He laughed and wiped a crumb off my lip, and when his breath quickened, I realized he was just as gone as I was.

I shivered and stared at his lips. God, they were luscious. I wanted to bite them. I wanted him to bite me back. Maybe get on that horse with him and let him tear my shirt off with his teeth. I imagined me sitting in front of him while his fingers skimmed my body. My clit. I bit back a moan.

"V? You with me?"

I jerked. "You really want to know what I'm thinking?"

He nodded.

"I'm trying to figure out in my head if it's possible to have sex on a horse."

He went utterly still. "And what did you decide?"

I sucked in a sharp breath. "That—that we'd better talk about something else."

He nodded.

"There's something I've been wanting to ask you," he said a few minutes later.

I smirked good-naturedly. "Is this about watching that *Star Wars* marathon with you? Because I'm not a sci-fi fan. Although if you give me a neck rub like last night, I might give in."

"No, this is serious."

My body pinged with awareness. "Oh?"

He stared straight ahead, curiously not meeting my gaze. "Briarwood Academy—my high school—is having a reunion, and I want you to go with me."

"Like a date?" My voice was breathless.

He rubbed his jaw and thought about it. "Do you want it to be a date?"

My heart banged in my chest. It felt like high school all over again, which was terribly ironic. "Do you?"

"Do dates kiss each other?"

I nodded. And more.

"Alright, I'd kiss you," he murmured.

"Oh." What did that mean?

He flashed me a grin. "It's still a few months away, but I've cleared my schedule so we can drive cross-country to Dallas. I'd like to spend some time with Leo and Nora when we're there. We can stay with them—or not. It's up to you. I can't wait for you to meet my niece, Gabby."

"Wait, you planned a driving trip because of my fear of flying? You want me to meet your family?"

He sent me a cocked eyebrow. "Duh."

Sweetness swept over me. "Thank you," I said simply. "Date or not, I'd love to go."

He shrugged, but it felt like something big had just happened.

We arrived at the cabin a bit later. Situated on a small hill, the rugged structure was secluded and quaint with a fire pit and even a big wooden swing mounted between two sturdy oak trees.

When we walked inside, however, we discovered a small problem.

Mila pursed her lips. "This is all wrong. The picture on the brochure showed four beds, not two."

I peeked my head in the first bedroom. Yep. One smallish bed. It was the same in the second bedroom.

Spider, who didn't seem concerned—who in fact looked pleased—spoke up. "I'm not cuddling with Sebastian on that tiny bed." He grinned at us broadly. "So which one of you birds is gonna keep me warm?"

Mila poked him in the arm. "Watch yourself, Clarence."

He blanched, his eyes on me and then back to her. "Mila, fuck, no one, and I mean no one knows my real name. Easy there, my love."

I chuckled. "Clarence? No wonder you kept that under wraps."

He strutted around the small den. "Spider suits me better. That's all. But you are now sworn to secrecy. You can't tell anyone, V."

"You called her *my love*," I felt compelled to add since no one else seemed to notice.

"I did?" Spider asked, a quizzical look on his face.

"Yes," we all said. Mila blushed.

"So." He took out a cig and lit it up. His hand trembled.

"Ugh, take your smart mouth and that cancer stick outside." Mila pushed at him until they were out the door.

Sebastian groaned as they left. "How much longer can I let them go on like this without saying anything?"

I sighed. It was obvious to everyone that they were into each other.

"Spider does seem calmer when she's around."

I tugged on his hand. "You can't control people or emotions."

He swept his tongue over his bottom lip as he gazed at me. "Tell me about it."

An hour later, no one mentioned the sleeping arrangements again as we pulled out the grill and built a bonfire. Spider and Sebastian cooked the burgers and Mila and I made a salad. We drank cold beer with stars above us as brilliant as diamonds.

"This is the best thing I've done in a long time," I told them softly, looking at each of them as I sat on our blanket and roasted a marshmallow in the diminishing fire.

Mila smiled as she snuggled with Spider. "I agree."

I took a big breath. "Guys, there's something I'd like to ask you tonight. All of you."

"What?" Sebastian said, easing over to sit next to me on the blanket.

I clasped my hands together. "One of the reasons I moved here was an orphanage my parents had been interested in sponsoring. I grew up helping them, and I don't want to stop just because they're gone."

"What a great way to honor your parents," Mila said.

I nodded. "So, the orphanage is gearing up for a big benefit gala, and I'm helping with the planning. I—I wanted to ask if you'd be willing to come and support me and be the entertainment? Just play a couple of songs? I know your other band guys are in Dallas on hiatus—"

Sebastian had a funny expression on his face as he looked at me. "Wait a minute—what's the name of this orphanage?"

"Lyons Place."

Silence fell as Spider and Sebastian looked at each other and then back at me.

Mila straightened up at the guys' odd expressions. "What's

going on? You guys look weird."

"Spider and I volunteer there."

I shook my head in bewilderment. "How is that even possible? That's crazy. It's one of several homes in LA. Did you know it was mine?"

Sebastian shook his head. "No. Just something about the place called to me. I saw the sign one day, and wanted to go in. We've been teaching guitar lessons there."

I licked my lips. "What a weird coincidence."

"It's the universe trying to get you two pussies together," Spider muttered.

Oh.

"I can help with the planning," Mila offered, as we all ignored Spider's remark. "I have a list of celebrities we can invite. Big spenders."

I grinned. "Thank you. I can't tell you how much it means to me."

"We'd love to help you with the gala, but there's one condition," Sebastian said.

"What?" I asked. My heart thudded and I don't even know why, except that I was reeling from knowing that he was already part of something that was important to me.

"I said I'd find you a gig, and I have. You play with us at the gala."

"But why would you want me to?"

"Because it's *you*, V, and I want you to be happy. I'd do anything for you. Don't you see that?" His voice was heavy with emotion.

Mila and Spider got up and murmured excuses about getting more marshmallows, and headed back to the cabin. I didn't think they'd be back.

I stared at Sebastian as he sat next to me. "Why am I so special to you?"

His finger started at my head and traced a line down between my eyes, over the slope of my nose, past my lips, my neck, and down to my pounding heart. "You've two sides to you, V. One wants to be the way you used to be, but the other side of you has found a new home. You're starting to shine—hell, sparkle. *I see it.* I want to see you shine on stage in front of an audience too."

How was it that he knew exactly what I needed to hear?

I leaned into him, and he leaned into me, both of us breathing in the other.

We sat like that, his fingers tracing little designs on my arm, his lips a hair's breadth from mine. My fingers itched to trace his lips, to pull him down to me, but it was a line I couldn't cross. Not if we were just friends.

After a while, he tugged a blanket around my shoulders. "I need to put you to bed," he whispered in my ear.

"I don't want to go to bed and neither do you. Plus, Spider and Mila are probably having sex in the cabin as we speak. We should sleep here. Together."

He stilled his hands, which had been rubbing my back. "What are you saying?"

I inhaled sharply. "That I want you, and I'll take you any way I can, even if it means just one night."

"You're on dangerous ground, V." His voice had deepened.

"I'm sick to death of tip-toeing around how bad I want you. I think you are too."

His fingers stroked my lips, rubbing across my upper lip and then my lower. "I don't want to ruin our friendship."

I captured his fingers. "Then kiss me and pretend it's a plain kiss, one that doesn't mean a thing."

His chest rose, distance building in his eyes. "I want you, but you'd regret us in the morning when things are back to normal."

Enough. I was tired of his push and pull. Tired of the longing looks he'd give me but then deny them. "Forget it. I'm not going to beg you to make love to me, Sebastian. If you want me, come and get me." I jerked up and strode off toward the large wooden swing near the two oak trees. Sturdy and made for two, it was the perfect place to vent. I sat down and leaned back to push off.

"Dammit, come back," he demanded from behind me. I shivered at the tinge of authority in his tone, every molecule in me wanting to turn around and run to him. I resisted and settled for pushing off again.

He walked over to me with intent, his broad shoulders blocking out the moon.

Sending me a searing look, he halted in front of me and pulled on the chain to stop my momentum.

I gasped. "What are you doing?"

He scowled. "Get off that swing, V, or I'll fuck you while you're on it."

And as if on cue, my core got wet for him. "Don't make a promise you won't keep," I said softly.

CHAPTER 14

"Even wrapped in sorrow, she lived in color."—Sebastian Tate

MY COMPOSURE CRACKED. WHICH WASN'T SURPRISING, considering the way she'd been prancing around in those tight jeans all day, talking about sex on a horse. My willpower had dissolved into dust. I was so screwed.

"Get off and face me," I told her. "Or are you all talk and no play?"

I put my hand out and helped her stand, her eyes wide as I tugged her against my chest and kissed her. I cradled her head with my hands and took what I'd wanted all day. She tasted like marshmallows and I groaned, needing more of her, more of *us*. Like a man dying of thirst in the desert, her lips and tongue were a fucking waterfall.

I kissed down her neck and nibbled and then sucked on the hollow of her throat. My hands moved to her shoulders, cupping them, and then moved down to play with the buttons on her shirt.

Her breath came in little gasps. "Sebastian?" she whispered as I tugged her shirt out of her jeans, pulled it off her head and tossed it on the ground.

I tweaked her nipples through her bra, making her hiss. "I'm going to do what I've wanted to since the first time I saw you. I'm going to make you mine—just like you want, V."

She shivered and I put my hand to her chest. "Your heart

is flying. Do you want me to stop? Because I'm about three seconds away from a point of no return with you. My cock is hard enough to chop wood, and we don't need anymore for the fire."

She sighed. "Please don't stop."

I reached behind her and took the bigger than normal swing seat and tossed it over the branches until it was raised, tugging on it to make sure it would hold.

"What's going on?"

Without answering, I turned back to her and pushed her bra down underneath her breasts, positioning them so I could lean in and lick one and then the other. I shoved them together and sucked hard, making her gasp out as she clutched me.

This is what she craved. Intensity. Consuming need. I'd sensed it in her from the moment she played, and I burned for her, my entire body throbbing, shaking with need. "I feel like I've walked away from you a thousand times. But not this time," I murmured.

She nodded and that was all the acquiescence I needed. I peeled my shirt off and tossed it with hers. I unzipped her jeans and shoved them down, my hands cupping her ass and squeezing. *God, she was beautiful.* "I love you in red, V," I said, fingering the lace of her panties.

With need riding me, I fell to my knees and kissed her stomach, my tongue delving in her navel. *Worshipping her.* I bit her hipbones and then sucked them gently as I eased her boots off.

She cried out my name beseechingly as I slipped my fingers inside her panties and burrowed inside, finding her hot and wet. Fuck, yeah. My fingers skimmed her pussy and then teased her entrance, her juices making it easy for me to slide in. I rolled her clit around as she squirmed to get more of me. "You been

144

thinking about me all day?" I said, my voice low, my breathing winded.

She nodded, her head tossed back as I slid my fingers in and out of her. "Yes," she ground out. "I wanted you on the ride. I wanted to sit in front of you on your horse while you did this until I came."

My heart raced, and my adrenaline shot sky high. I needed more. I needed her riding my cock.

But first . . .

I eased her panties down and she stepped out of them. "Sit back on the swing and spread your legs," I rasped out. "Scoot your body forward, V, so I can put my mouth on you."

She sat down and parted her legs for me, her eyes glowing. "Make me burn for you."

I cupped her breasts and raked my eyes over her, soaking it in. She looked gorgeous and ready, her eyes heavy-lidded, her lips plump from where I'd kissed her. I placed her hands on the chains of the swing and positioned her legs further apart until she was spread before me beautifully, her body glistening for me.

Desperation drove me. I had to have her taste, her smell in my mouth.

On my knees, I pulled the swing forward with one hand and pressed her hot core against my stiff tongue. The fingers of my other hand explored her gently, even as my tongue pillaged and took control. She writhed and leaned back, bucking to give me more access. Desire owned me as I delved into her, my fingers finding her sweetest spot. I rubbed her wetness around, some soft strokes, some more insistent, her little cries driving me on. She was letting go, her body flushed and straining to come.

"I want to touch you," she gasped out.

"Be still," I rumbled against her. "Going to give you the

145

best orgasm you've ever had." My hand tightened on the swing, yanking her closer. My tongue and lips devoured her as I rubbed her harder, working her clit and then moving away to tease her honeyed entrance.

She panted, a bead of sweat dripping down her forehead.

"Wider," I demanded, nudging her legs apart more. "More, V, I need more."

She bit her lip and whimpered as she edged lower and spread her legs even more, her hips jerking as she tried to get more friction. "Please, Sebastian."

I lifted my head and gazed into her eyes. "You're beautiful, V. I want to remember you like this forever. Begging for my touch."

She squirmed and keened. "Just make me come, or I'll kill you."

Heat zipped up my spine. "Hang on, baby." I lowered my head, taking her sex hard with an open mouth, my fingers probing and twisting rapidly. She called out my name and stiffened, her tits quivering as she came hard against me. I held on tightly, embracing her hips with my arm and watching her face as she let go. Moments went by as she clenched and unclenched her muscles around my finger, milking me. I continued to touch her, making it last, wanting my dick in her so bad I could cry. Nothing in the world mattered but this. *Her.*

Finally her hips slowed and she sat up. "How was that?" I whispered against her nipples, my lips unable to stop tasting her skin. She was addictive.

She stared at me and the beauty of the moment blew me away, because her face was so open—with an unnamed emotion on it.

"You on your knees . . . your mouth on me. I may die now,"

she whispered softly.

"Good. But we aren't done yet." I stood up and unzipped my jeans and shoved them off. My tight underwear came next. I tugged my boots off and rolled on a condom I'd taken from my pocket. I stood before her and fisted my cock. I let my heavy gaze slide over her breasts and I reached out to thumb her nipple. I growled, "Now grip those chains and lean back in that swing and get ready."

She obliged with wide eyes, and I pulled her closer and kissed her long and hard, my mouth taking her soft lips. I moved down to her neck and shoulders and to her breast, which I suckled like a needy kitten, pushing her breasts together and taking as much as I could in my mouth. "You taste good, V."

She trembled and pulled my head up. "Sebastian, look, I'm feeling so much here, and it isn't just sex. It's—"

I got her. "You're everything in a woman I've ever wanted, V. It scares me too, and I don't know what it means—"

Fuck. I lost every thought in my head when she bit my nipple.

I cupped her ass with one hand and pulled the swing toward me with the other until I'd seated myself deep inside her. She whimpered, and I tossed my head back and wanted to howl at the damn moon.

I took her, watching my cock glide in and out.

"Harder. Yes, yes, yes," she said as I plunged in and out of her, using the swing to mechanize my movements. To own her.

She wriggled around and locked her legs on my hips, trying to get as much of me in her as she could. Desire surged through every vein in my body as my cock pounded her. *V.*

But then why did I feel so damn moody and dark with desperation?

I hissed in her ear. "You're mine, V. And I know it sounds possessive and caveman, but tonight, I don't give a fuck. Don't think about Geoff or anything but my cock in you. Got it?" I tempered those words by sucking on her earlobe.

She drank me in as I hovered above her. "Yes . . . so good, so good, so good," she moaned at each thrust.

I repositioned my stance and lowered the swing a tad, pushing in and then out, sliding over her clit and then plunging deep inside her. I tossed my head back, trying to keep it together, but knowing I was going to go over the cliff soon. It had been too long since I'd been with a girl, and this was V.

"Touch yourself, V. I'm dying to, but my hands are full," I muttered, gritting my teeth for control. She touched her slit, flicking her fingers. Slow. Fast.

"I don't want to stop," I growled out.

We were lost. My skin tingled. My head floated.

I plunged in her wetness, the sounds of our sex, my grunts, her whimpers . . . it all crashed and my cock swelled painfully as I came hard. My body pulsed, and I roared into the night.

Without pausing, I fell to my knees and took her in my mouth again. She screamed, her hands twisting the chain as she came hard, her pussy pulsing against my hands and mouth. After a while, she leaned up and sagged against me as we held each other for a few moments, neither of us able to speak.

I let go of the swing, swept her limp body up in my arms and took her back to the fire and the blanket and lay her down. My head was dizzy and my heart was thundering. I felt on top of the fucking world.

But . . .

What the hell was I going to do now?

CHAPTER 15

"You never love the same way twice, but the love of a lifetime only comes once."—from the journal of Violet St. Lyons

E EASED ME DOWN ON THE BLANKET AND PRESSED A KISS TO MY forehead as if I were a piece of fine china, his gentleness a sharp contrast to the fierceness of his lovemaking. He pulled the ends of the blanket around us while my eyes bored into his, searching for his soul.

Could he tell that things had been irrevocably changed between us?

I glanced up just as a brilliant light raced overhead, zipping through the heavens and leaving a glittering trail. I took it as a sign, and my mouth parted as I recognized the beautiful truth. No matter what happened after this, he and I *were* meant to had met. We were destined for this moment.

"A shooting star," I breathed.

His full lips tilted up, his gaze tender as he tweaked my nose. "You're welcome. Always knew I had the heavens in my pocket. Wanna see a comet next?"

Feeling oddly euphoric, I slapped his shoulder while he pretended to be hurt. "Hey, that's no way to treat the master of the universe."

I chuckled and traced my finger around the Superman tattoo on his chest. "You know, I was born the night the Violette-Sells comet went across the Manhattan skyline. My parents joked that I was lucky it wasn't the Hyakutake-Bayshi comet or else my name might have been super weird. My dad . . . he loved to point out different constellations to me, especially if we were in another country where the view of the sky was different. He said we're all made up of dust from the universe. We're all born from stars."

"Sounds like a good line for a song."

I looked up at him. "Will you write a song about me? About tonight and what we did?" There was no mistaking the heaviness of my question or the hesitation in my voice.

"V, I could write a million songs about you, and none of them would have anything to do with having sex with you, but everything to do with how unbelievably mysterious you are. You're like a rich red wine, dark and bittersweet and so damn intoxicating that I want to guzzle you down."

A puff of air escaped my mouth. Since the moment we'd met, he'd gotten the essence of who I was.

A look of yearning crossed his face. "I wish I could have met your parents, to tell them *thank you* for having you and just, I don't know, making you *who* you are. My parents would have adored you, by the way. Music was everything to our family. Plus, you're hot. Dad always liked brunettes."

"Are brunettes your favorite too?" I said as I kissed his bicep, letting my tongue drift over his arm and up his shoulder where I traced his lion tattoo. My hands drifted down to his length, stroking him. He hardened immediately.

"V, you make me crazy," he murmured, his hands slipping through my hair to pull my lips to his for a long kiss. I moaned into his mouth.

He pulled back to stare at me with a sheepish smile. "God, I want you again, but my legs are still quivering."

I laughed. "I don't think many women get to have sex on

a swing. Huh, I guess we've ruined that poor thing for the next people who come here. Maybe we should take it with us? I've never had sex anywhere except in a bed—"

He put his finger to my lips. "Don't. Please. I don't want an image of you with someone else in my head."

"Why?" I couldn't stop the question.

His lips tightened. "Because it makes me want to fucking beat the shit out of something—namely Geoff." He seemed to gather himself and took a deep breath. "Do you still love him?"

"I do, but not in the way you think. At one time, I thought I'd spend the rest of my life with him, but people change. He's part of my past—and I hope someday part of my future as a friend. There's not a lot of people who knew my parents the way he did."

A muscle in his jaw clenched, and I scrambled to explain how Geoff was part of my heart yet he didn't own it. "Maybe it's kinda like your sister-in-law Nora. You love her but it's platonic."

"Nope. I never dated her. We never even kissed. Not even *close* to the same." He sighed as he stared back up at the sky. "I don't want to talk about Geoff. Tell me some of the things your dad taught you about the stars."

"Okay," I said, letting it go. I showed him the constellation Leo the Lion. Raising my hands, I traced the triangle of eastern stars that made up the tail and hindquarters. I pointed out Regulus, the sparkling blue-white star. "Because Regulus is the brightest, it symbolizes the lion's heart. Some of the ancient astronomers called it the King Star."

He smiled. "If I'm a king, will you be my queen tonight?"

My stomach fluttered. "What happens tomorrow?"

He turned to look at me. "I don't want to think about tomorrow right now. I just want to hold you while you tell me stories about stars and comets and whatever else you've got tucked up there." He smoothed his fingers over my forehead. "I like hearing you talk about your parents because I don't think you have in a long time. It—it makes me feel close to you—which is something I've never had with a girl. Shit, that's stupid." He shook his head.

"No, it's beautiful. I feel the same. I've been barely breathing and now for the first time, I feel like I can take a deep breath. You do that to me."

"Take all your deep breaths with me, V," he whispered.

My stomach dipped. He spoke like a man in love, but perhaps he said that to all the girls.

We stared at each other, and I don't know what he was thinking, but as for me . . . well, *I was falling in love*. Perhaps the emotion had been there for a while, but it had taken the shooting star to make me see the truth. The intensity between us became sharper, and I reached out to touch his face, wanting to open up to him—but he broke our gaze and looked hurriedly away. I sighed.

He snuggled me close and changed gears. "Okay, let's hear more about how majestic this lion is. Was he as great as I am?"

I smiled and shook my head. "You are so full of shit, but as it happens, Hercules killed the lion and to commentate the victory, Zeus flung his body into the sky—hence the constellation."

"Poor dude. At least everyone knows who he is." He smiled. "Got anymore stories?"

"I'm not boring you?"

"You're fascinating, V." He pushed a strand of hair behind my ear. "This—this is the happiest I've been since I moved to LA."

My heart stuttered at those words, but I pushed on, not commenting.

I nodded and went on to tell him about the other names of the stars I knew until finally I grew sleepy. He did too, his breathing in sync with mine as we held each other. Once he went to sleep, I gazed at him, my eyes tracing the lines of his face and memorizing them. I feared we'd never be this close again.

I sent one final glance up at the stars and rested my head on his shoulder.

We slept as the heavens watched.

❧

His lone finger traced a line from my shoulder blade down my spine, over the crest of my buttocks, and then back to my opposite shoulder blade. Slow and easy as if he had all the time in the world.

I kept the rise and fall of my chest steady and pretended to be asleep as he caressed me. He kissed the top of my shoulders, the puff of his warm breath followed by the gentleness of his nose as he inhaled my skin. Again, he outlined the shape, starting at the top, moving down the center of my back and then back up.

I shivered when I realized what he was writing. *V.*

His voice was gruff from sleep. Husky. Sexy. "You awake?"

My eyes blinked open just as the first peek of sunlight crested the trees on the hill in front of us. "It's dawn," I said, not masking the sadness in my voice.

He pulled on my shoulder, but I resisted, my heart still needing a minute to process that this had been a one-night thing.

"V, turn around." His hand went to the curve of my hip and tugged. "Look at me."

"No, I can't. Not yet. I'm going to get up and find my clothes and go shower." But I didn't move.

A few beats of silence went by and then some rustling as he stood up. "If you won't face me, then I'll face you." He walked around to my side and bent down to look at me.

I gasped. "Put some clothes on," I hissed, darting a glance back at the cabin.

"It's not even six. Spider is probably passed out, and Mila likes to sleep. We're alone. Plus, you like looking at me." He grinned and flexed a bicep.

There was that.

My eyes flared as he took my hand and pulled me up from the blanket. "What are you doing? I'm naked," I said between my teeth chattering, and it wasn't even that cold, but it was just him. Being this close to him. Loving him and now losing him.

"Our night isn't over," he said.

"I disagree." I nodded at the obvious sunrise. "Even the birds are chirping."

"Until I see the full sun with my eyes, it's not over. *We* are not over."

"Oh, so we're just going to disregard the obvious fact that it *is* the next day?"

"You talk way too much, V." And then he kissed me hard, his tongue exploring my mouth as his hands cupped my ass and pulled me against his already hard cock.

Like a magnet to steel, his lips devoured mine, eating me up, taking everything I had until I was breathless. But I didn't need air. All I needed was him. His lips, his tongue, his teeth. I returned his fire, my hands clasped around his neck, hanging on.

"You. This. The sunrise. It's fucking perfect," he said gutturally as I went to my knees and took him in my mouth. He was too big to take in at once, so I worked him in gently, licking the sides, pressing kisses to his skin. My tongue dabbed at his head and sucked his length, stroking the shaft with my hands. I moaned against him, making him quiver.

"I don't want to come like that, V. I want inside you." He pulled me up and swept me up in his arms and carried me over to the swing and set me down on my feet.

"More swing sex?" I murmured as he ran his mouth down my neck and captured my nipple between his lips and pulled.

"You complaining?" he mumbled against my breast.

"Never," I squeaked incoherently as he kissed his way down to my stomach. He lavished attention on me with his mouth, finding the soft skin behind my knees, the dimples on my lower back. He worshipped me, pleasing only me, and I watched, stroking his hair, my hands tracing his tattoos. My heart ached to tell him how I felt, but I was scared.

Later after I was a quivering mess, he stood and nodded at the swing. "Put your hands on the chains and bend over."

I blinked. "What? Are you going to spank me?"

His eyes went heavy-lidded. "Do you want me to? You like that?"

"No. Maybe? I don't know." I felt a flush start at my toes and work its way up to my face.

He chuckled at my embarrassment and kissed me gently. "V, all I want right now is to fuck you from behind."

"Why?" My heart thundered at the image.

"So I can see every detail of you wrapped around my cock and use my hands—anywhere I want."

I grasped the sides and bent over, presenting my backside to him. He let out a low groan and shuffled around, taking a few steps back to look at me. Then, he moved forward and ran his hands down my spine and back up, tracing my name again.

His chest heaved. *"V,"* he said softly, saying my name like a benediction.

I watched over my shoulder as he curved his hand over my bottom and slid his finger inside me. I closed my eyes. *Yes, yes, yes.* Heat flooded my face, and I cried out his name, my body going limp, moving with the steady rhythm of his hand. My body tingled, needing more, needing him in me.

My eyes flew open when he spread my legs further apart, his fingers ghosting over my clit and then easing back inside me. "You're so ready . . . you make me drunk with need," he said in a gravelly voice.

"Hurry," I said. "Please don't tease me."

He scrambled around in the pocket of his jeans, his hands visibly trembling until he found what he wanted and rolled the condom on. He kissed my lower back, his scruff the perfect roughness. "I should take you back to the blanket, and make love to you there, but I can't."

I shivered. "Yes, here." *Anywhere.* I let out a sharp moan as he lined up behind me and slid in, my wetness and the angle helping him go deeper than he'd been last night. He stirred around inside me and then started a slow pumping. I bent my head to watch as our bodies melded. His hands were busy too, ravaging my body, spreading me and touching me in taboo places I'd never dreamed, his fingers knowing just the right thing, just the perfect touch to make me whimper with need. He stoked my desire, he built it up and up, igniting me until I wanted to scream.

"Never like this before, V. Never," he growled as he held on to my hips and pumped, his tempo speeding up.

Sensation built. Fire burned. *I loved.*

Fireworks went off in my head, and I called his name

when I went over. His own body tightened and swelled, the friction the perfect balance of pleasure and pain. He roared, the noise reverberating against my skin as he bent over and buried his face in my neck.

Our hearts beat in sync, nature hummed, and the world was *right*.

Panting, I gazed back at him and realized that fear had chased me for too long when all I needed to do was be brave. *Just this one time.*

"I love you," I whispered. "Sebastian, I love you, I love you, I love you."

With every molecule, every atom, every tiny piece of me. Insanely. Madly. Completely. The truth was, he'd sparked life in me the day I saw him move in, and I'd tried to harden my heart against love, but in the end my dad's sacrifice had been too loud to stifle. Sebastian's pull toward me had been too strong, his connection too visceral.

I held on to the chains, chest heaving as he withdrew and took several of his own deep breaths. Finally, he came around to face me, unclasped my hands from the chains and gathered me in his arms. "Thank you, V." And then he kissed me. Sweetly.

Oh.

We dressed and walked hand-in-hand back to the blanket where he got a fire going. As the seconds stretched into minutes, and he didn't comment on my confession, my shoulders tightened and cement settled in my stomach.

"Do you have anything to say about what I said to you earlier?" I asked a bit later as we packed up our backpacks for the trip back down the mountain. I tried to keep my voice light, but I was hurting.

He paused, a muscle working in his cheek, as if what he was about to say was difficult. "No."

And I saw that we were done. Our *night* was over.

ღ

We rode back down the canyon the next day, a more subdued bunch than the day before. Spider and Mila seemed out of sorts, and Sebastian was unusually quiet. Both he and Spider had ridden off ahead of us to get back to the stables—something about calling Harry to check on the latest. It hurt to see him so distant. My body still vibrated at the memory of how he'd taken me.

No regrets, I told myself.

Mila rode up next to me, her glare on Spider's horse as it turned the bend ahead of us.

Ouch. Someone else was in the doghouse this morning. "Everything okay between you and Spider?"

She squirmed in her saddle. "We had this huge argument last night about Dovey—that's his first love from BA."

"What happened?" I asked.

"It's funny, I knew him in high school, but was never attracted to him. Mostly because I was intimidated by his bleached-out hair and tats. He even dressed all Goth with chains and piercings. But the one person he loved was Dovey Beckham, and she broke him."

"Yikes, she sounds like a bitch. Will I get to meet her at the reunion?"

Mila nodded. "She isn't, though. She's sweet and worked hard to hang in there with all the rich girls at BA. Anyway, in the end, when her adoptive mother got sick, she chose Cuba to be with—the guy who'd broken her heart the year before. Spider was left out." Her shoulders drooped. "It's just, we're complete opposites. His tattoos alone should scare me, but I want *him*. Am I crazy?"

"Something in you is drawn to him . . . you can't control that. Maybe you'd like Geoff? I can always set you up?"

She let out a squeak. "Oh God, Spider hates him." Her eyes flicked to me. "Oops, sorry. He was your fiancé at one time, so he must have some good points."

"He's a good guy. I think Spider and Sebastian brought out the worst in him."

She studied me. "Getting off the subject of me, either wild-cats were mating last night outside the cabin, or you got lucky."

I gripped the reins. "I told him I loved him, and he—he just clammed up."

Her eyes hardened. "Tate men are notoriously pig-headed. I suggest you play dirty if you want him, V. Of course, I gladly volunteer my services to make him jealous or pick you out a sexy outfit . . ." She snapped her fingers. "Wait, there's this butt model you should meet. He was an extra on the set when we filmed one of the music videos. Anyway, his name is Baxter, and he's likely gay—aren't all the hot ones?—but who really cares about that when his bum is tight enough to bounce a quarter off of? He's an ex-football player from Iowa and as country as a Blake Shelton song. He'd make some great eye candy. Want me to call him?" She fished out her phone from her saddlebag and wiggled her eyebrows at me.

"Does he like to dance?" I hadn't danced since my prep school dances.

Her eyes glowed. "Can he dance? *Can he dance?* Hello? He was *in* a video. He's got moves like Jagger."

"I don't know. It seems childish to flaunt a guy in front of Sebastian."

She flicked her reins at me. "Shut the feck up. Hasn't he rubbed your nose in his and Blair's affair? Make him pay, V, make him pay. For all womankind. Plus, you need the cheering up—and maybe I do too. We'll show those two pinheads that rode off and left us that all we need is each other. Girl Power." She clapped, and even though my heart ached, I laughed. Mila might look as prim as a schoolgirl out on a field trip, but inside she had the heart of a beast.

CHAPTER 16

"For two thousand dollars, I could get a sex-swing installed. But V was the only one I wanted to use it with."—Sebastian Tate

"That's awesome, Leo. I can't wait to see the new digs when I get to Dallas in September," I said to my cell as I strolled with Spider and Vilma Lopez, a journalist from *Rock Indie Today*. We just finished the photo shoot and were headed to Rio's in Beverly Hills for our lunch interview.

Leo chuckled. "Yeah, it's bigger than the Taj Mahal. Nora's got a giant office for her clothing line business, and I ended up with the smaller one—of course. We've got a huge theatre room, an Olympic-Sized pool—even Gabby's room is unbelievable." He paused. "This is probably boring as shit to you. You're the one with all the excitement . . . gearing up for a movie role, working on the new album—"

"No, I do want to hear about it." Plus, I didn't want to tell him that I didn't get the part.

"Yeah?"

He loved talking about his family, and I grinned even though he couldn't see me. "Spill the beans, man. Tell it all."

He settled in, his deep voice describing life at Chez Tate. "Nora went over the top with the nursery. She had this artist come out and paint these constellations and unicorns on the wall—it's fairytale land in her room. I'll be upfront with you— Gabby is spoiled rotten. She gets whatever she wants between

161

me and Nora and Aunt Portia. I mean, she's one, but she runs the house."

I laughed, and we chatted a bit more until he put Nora on.

"How's this V chick doing? I hope she's ready for questions, because I want to know all about the girl that Lion Boy is bringing home. Frankly, I'm shocked you'd even bring her back to BA and around all those crazy people we went to high school—"

"About that. I'm not sure if she's coming." We hadn't talked in the three days, not since the camping trip. I cleared my throat. "She's—I don't know—it's weird right now."

She got quiet and I could imagine her standing in her new house, narrowed eyes, trying to suss me out from two thousand miles away. A notorious people watcher, she had a big brain, and her favorite pastime was figuring out what made people tick.

She said, "I'm hearing some uncertainty in your voice. What's going on? Do I need to come to LA and kick some girl's ass? Or are *you* the one with the problem? Hmmm, come on, you can tell your stepmom."

I groaned. "Just because you're married to the man who raised me does not make me your stepson. Just *ewwww*." I paused. "But back to V—we got physical and things are off."

"Which is code for you had sex, and now you don't know how to handle it," she said. "Typical."

I didn't want to get into this. "Just put Gabby on, will you?"

She laughed. "Fine, avoid the issue—just like your brother—although I have trained him in the past few years to talk about his feelings . . ." she trailed off and I heard muffled laughter and then silence.

"Nora?"

I could hear rustling sounds—and then sighs.

"Are you getting busy with Leo while I'm on the phone with

you?" I called out.

From next to me, Spider did a lewd gesture with his hands and Vilma's eyebrows went up. Meh. It was Leo and Nora and they were known to be lusty.

"Nora, I'm hanging up if you don't say anything."

Her disembodied voice came through. "Okay. *Enough.* Stop kissing me there, Leo." She giggled.

I shook my head. "Get a damn room and put Gabby on."

"Okay, okay, here she is," Nora said, and I heard Gabby breathing into the phone. I went into *crazy uncle mode,* as Spider called it, and started in with some baby talk and then sang the "Superman" song for her. It was our thing. We passed people on the street who stared, but it didn't slow me down. I pictured her in Nora's arms, clutching the phone to her head, her blue eyes—which were just like mine and Leo's—as big as saucers as she hung on to my every word.

I said my goodbyes when we were led to our table at the Rio. We settled in and ordered drinks. I got a beer and Spider ordered a double shot of Jack.

Vilma began her interview as we ate. A pretty Latino with long dark hair and nice curves, Spider's eyes kept drifting over her assets. Thinking of Mila, I barely resisted the urge to kick him under the table,

"Our tag line for the cover is going to be *The Best in Indie.*" Vilma said. "It's quite an honor for the Vital Rejects to be on the list, and I just wanted to say that when this story came across my desk, I got giddy. Your music is one of my personal favorites. Can you tell me what's in store for the band next? Is it true there's a movie in the works?" she asked us.

Uh, no.

I cleared my throat. "We're working in the studio on a new

album. We don't have definite tour dates yet, but they are coming. As far as movie rumors, we've not signed any deals." In fact, I'd been toying with the idea of ditching Harry and looking for other representation.

She scribbled in her notebook and then looked back up. "And the question everyone wants to know is are you still dating Blair Storm? You haven't been seen in public since the *Hollywood Insider* ran photos of you with a dark-haired girl. Can you tell me more about who this girl is and is she someone special?"

My mouth dried. I knew the tough questions were coming, and I could handle reporters, especially ones who tended to blush every time I looked at them, but this time I froze. I realized I wanted to be seen with V in public—even if we were just friends.

I must have waited too long to answer. Spider jumped in. "Blair is such an incredibly beautiful person, both inside and out, and one of our dearest friends, especially mine. She is an inspiration to me." He leaned in. "In fact, she's donating fifty thousand dollars to the Lyons Place Orphanage here in LA. You *must* ask her about it. Her fans would love to hear how Miss Storm supports the needy." Yeah, Spider had a vindictive streak.

Vilma wrote in her book furiously while I just shook my head.

"So you and Blair are just friends?" she asked.

She wasn't going to let it go. I licked my lips. "Blair's a very special person in my life." Special like a lunatic. "And that's all you need to know."

"What about the Mystery Girl, Sebastian? You've never come out and talked about her. Why all the secrecy?"

I stiffened in my seat, setting my beer down carefully as I eyed Vilma. No one was going to harass V.

Vilma picked up on my body cues. "Does that question upset you?"

I smiled tightly. "Of course not. The so-called Mystery Girl is not anyone we know. She happened to get sick at the restaurant and I helped her. That's all."

"He's a fucking hero. That's what you need to publish." Spider waggled his eyes at her and ran a finger down her arm. "Now, when are you and I going to have drinks—alone? I need some advice on this new tattoo I want to get—maybe a brown recluse on my arse. What do you think? Would you be scared of that?"

Usually, I groan at Spider's pick-up lines, but he was flirting to save my ass.

Everything zoomed out when I happened to glance across the restaurant and see V at a table near the window. I did a double take. She sat with Wilson and a thirtyish-looking man who was currently staring at V like she was his chocolate soufflé.

I inhaled sharply and jerked my eyes back. I didn't want to cause any undue attention her way, but why was she here and who was she with? Wilson was fine—he was in his sixties—but the other guy . . .

Even from here, I could see that she looked beautiful. Her hair was wild as it fell on either side of her angular face. She'd gone heavy on the lipstick and mascara and it suited her. As I watched, she turned to Wilson and I got a load of what she was wearing—a slinky as hell silver top that plunged deep between her breasts. You could plainly see the curve of her tits . . . that I'd sucked and loved and held in my hands just three days ago. I felt my face go red with anger. One thing was certain, she'd evolved since the days when I'd perched on my patio and spied on her.

No more lonely girl who wore band shirts and ate cheese

puffs and Oreos.

She laughed suddenly, the sound clear as a bell, and all the memories from the camping trip came back. *She'd told me she loved me.* And yeah, my chest had seized at the thought of saying it back—because first off, it would be a lie, and secondly, I had never said those words to a girl.

Since then, she hadn't returned my texts, nor had she played her violin outside.

Yep. V was pissed at me. And she had no fucking right.

I glared at them. Then why was she in such a good mood when I was miserable? I sipped on my beer and pretended to eat as Spider and Vilma kept the interview going. I jumped in a few times, but mostly I let Spider handle it.

"... mate, you okay?" Spider's voice penetrated my thoughts a while later.

I looked at his face, down at my half-eaten sandwich and at the empty chair next to him. "She's gone?"

Shit, I was out of it.

He nodded. "I saw V, too, so I told Vilma we had another appointment—I'm meeting her for a drink later tonight. I told her I'd give her more scoop then." He paused, flicking his eyes over at V. "You wanna get out of here? I'm itching for a cig."

"Thanks for covering for me."

He shrugged. "Consider it me saying I'm sorry for messing with Mila. You were right . . . I'm not boyfriend material. I can't be good for a girl." He cleared his throat, a surprisingly serious look on his face. "We never had sex, you know. Third base, yeah, and there was that time in the pool—"

"Stop right there." I held up my hand. "Keep your dirty deeds to yourself. Just stay away from her unless you want to put a ring on it." I stood up and tossed back the rest of my beer.

He stood and slipped on his blue leather jacket. "Okay. I'm headed to get a haircut. Steve's holding a spot for me. You wanna go?"

"You go on. I'm going to say hi to V and Wilson." And find out who that guy was.

Spider fidgeted. "Don't make a scene, man."

I reared back. "Holy shit, what alternate universe is this? You covered my ass at lunch, you did the right thing by ending it with Mila, and now you're telling *me* to not make a scene? The guy who smashed up five guitars on stage last year alone?"

A corner of his mouth quirked up. "I paid for those guitars and the crowd fucking loved it. You know girls fancy me when I get all beastly."

I groaned. "Whatever. Tell Steve and his girls hi from me, and I'll be in for a cut soon."

He left and I headed over to V's table.

I knew the moment she realized I was there, because her eyes flared wide and a flush started at the base of her throat and went all the way up.

I nodded at Mr. Wilson. An older man, I'd watched V come in and out of his house a few times when I'd been driving by, and I guess he was her only friend besides us.

Wilson indicated the brown-haired, suave-looking guy who sat next to V. "This is my son Mark Wilson, Sebastian."

I reached over the table, shook hands, and exchanged pleasantries. Was my handshake super firm—to the point that he winced? Maybe.

"He works for Paramount as a studio head," Wilson added proudly.

Perfect. Not only was he related to Wilson, but he was successful. I tried to not glower—or bare my teeth at him. It was hard because his eyes were glued to her breasts, and he was sitting too fucking close to her.

"Would you like to join us?" V asked. Her face was devoid of emotion, and I should have been glad about that—that she was okay with us—but instead it just made me more antsy.

I rubbed my mouth. "No, but thank you. I just ate actually. We had a lunch interview."

"Oh. I hope it went well," she said coolly and then sipped on a glass of water, her tongue darting out to lick the drops off her bottom lip.

My ribs got tight, and I shoved my hands in my pockets to keep from losing it. I wanted her. Even here in this crowded restaurant.

How the hell were we supposed to just be friends?

"I hear you may be in the next Hing movie, Sebastian," Mark said, and I swiveled my eyes to him. "It's a rare musician who can convince that bastard to give them a chance." He smiled.

I blinked. Was the asshole sincere? "Actually, I think Hing has gone in a new direction." I shrugged to blow it off.

V set her glass down rather loudly. Her face was white.

Mr. Wilson darted his eyes between me and V, a worried frown on his face, and I knew it was time to leave, but first . . .

"V, uh, may I speak to you alone? There's something I forgot to mention earlier . . ." My voice trailed off. I stood there like an idiot.

Her hands twitched on top of the table. "Sure." She rose up. "Excuse me, gentlemen, I'll be *right* back."

She came around the table and I bit back a groan. Her silver top was nothing compared to the short black leather shorts she wore on her long legs. On her feet were a pair of tall, black shiny boots. It was enough to make me squirm.

"What are you doing . . . and where are we going?" she hissed as I led her back to the busy kitchen at Rio's. Waiters, managers, and chefs scurried in and out as we weaved through a corridor of ovens and prep areas. No one stopped us, and since it was the height of the lunch rush, I figured we had a good chance of skating by.

"Act like you own the place. It works for me," I said, nodding at a server as we headed toward the back.

"You're insane." She sent a wild-eyed look around. "If someone figures out who I am, Blair will crucify you in the media."

I got to the back of the kitchen expecting to see a back door, but there wasn't one. All I saw were rows of walk-in coolers. I must have went the wrong way. I strode up to the pastry chef who was decorating some cakes.

"Sir?" I asked and slipped him a wad of hundreds and patted him on the arm. "Need to use your walk-in cooler for five minutes. You good with that?"

"Absolutely." He pocketed the money in his white chef outfit.

I winked at him. "Keep this between us, and I'll eat here for the next week, and sing nothing but praises for your cakes—" I looked at his nametag "—Carl."

He grinned. "No problem, Mr. Tate. We protect our customers."

"Can you make sure we have some privacy?"

"Damn straight," he said. "Loved your last album, by the way. Think you can get me some tickets to your next show?"

"Whatever, man. It's yours."

Not waiting any longer, I opened the cooler and pulled her inside and shut the door. We were surrounded by rows of cold beer, boxes of lettuce, and big jugs of mayonnaise. Not the most romantic place.

She tossed her hands up in the air. "What the hell is wrong with you? You're acting like a crazy person. You interrupt my lunch like a caveman and practically pull me back to this cold refrigerator with you—"

"Are you on a date with Mark? Dressed like that?" I glowered.

She tilted her chin up. "He's a nice guy, and maybe I wouldn't be opposed if he asked me out—after all, I'm not tied down to anyone . . . not Geoff or *you*. But for your information, I'm here to discuss the gala. Both are big contributors to the event and very interested in providing—"

I kissed her. I told myself it was to shut her up, but the truth was she was so damn beautiful. And her nipples were like beacons in her shirt. I wanted my hands on them.

She pushed at my chest—until I stuck my tongue in her mouth and she let out a little whimper and clawed at my shoulders to pull me close.

It seemed I wasn't the only one who was jonesing for another go.

Her tongue battled with mine, and we escalated fast. I eased her back against the wall, sliding my hand inside her shirt and squeezing her breast. My lips followed my hand, sucking her nipple through her silk shirt. She clutched my hair and moaned.

"I want my mouth all over you, V. Again. I can't get enough."

She let out a shaky breath as her hand went to my jeans. She unzipped them, slipped inside and stroked my cock, her soft fingers ghosting over the head.

"I can't quit thinking about you," I groaned as she cupped my balls and squeezed. "All damn day you're in my head . . . all fucking night I'm dreaming of you."

"Good," she breathed.

We were desperate. Hot. Needy.

Hurry, hurry ran through my mind.

I just wanted her.

Just one more time and that would be it. One last time. *I promise*, I told myself, and then we'd just be friends.

"Why haven't you called me back? Why are you ignoring me?" I said against her neck, my teeth taking a bite and then my lips soothing it.

No answer. But her hands clenched around my cock, making me hiss.

"Fine. I know what you want," I said and kissed her mouth hard, my hands pulling at her hair. She returned it with her own fire, her teeth and lips ravaging me. We tore into each other, anger and lust and jealousy and pent-up animal need driving us.

I panted. Out of control. "Spread your legs, V."

She did, and I propped one of her legs up on a box of beer as I slipped a finger in her underwear and skimmed across her pussy. All the blood in my body went straight to my cock. "You're so wet for me. I need you—right now. This is all I can think about. You. Me. Fucking."

She stopped unbuttoning my shirt and shoved at me.

I stumbled back. *What?*

"That's what this is to you, isn't it? I'm just another girl. In fact, this probably isn't the first time you've had sex *in a refrigerator*," she yelled at me as she yanked down her skirt. "You saw me with Mark, and you just had to come over and put your mark on me—no pun intended." She pointed at the wet spot on her shirt.

"No, it wasn't like that." It was. "Shit, V, it feels like we aren't even friends anymore." I tugged at my hair. "I'm sorry, it was my fault at the canyon. I couldn't say no to you, and now I want you again. You looked so good and—"

"Just stop. I told you I wouldn't regret it, and I don't. It was the best sex I've ever had, okay. Is that what you want to hear?"

Hell yeah.

She continued. "But—but I need to protect myself. You have the power to hurt me, Sebastian. We're friends and nothing else from now on."

Fuck. I scrubbed my face. What was I doing? If I couldn't love her, then at least I could leave her alone.

With my heart hurting, I nodded. "Fine. Are you free tomorrow to go to the studio and work on the set list for the gala? You are still playing with us, right?" I just needed her near me.

She straightened her hair and clothes. "But first, we're going to walk out of here like we didn't just nearly have sex on a box of Bud Light."

CHAPTER 17

"In the end I'm here to tell you that I love comets and fairy dust too much to let life pass me by."—from the journal of Violet St. Lyons

THE NEXT WEEK, I SPENT TIME IN THE STUDIO WITH SEBASTIAN AND Spider working on the song I was going to play with them at the gala. He'd chosen his breakout hit "Superman", only he'd slowed it down so I could open the number before Spider's guitar riff kicked in. It made me jittery and queasy to sit there and work with two seasoned musicians critiquing me, but it wasn't enough to send me into a blind panic.

The air was charged between us, though, with stolen glances and brushes of our skin. I did my best to give him plenty of leeway and not be alone with him. Like a rubberband that's about to snap, the tension threatened to drive me insane.

Just yesterday in the studio, I'd been leaning over the music stand to find my notes and when I raised back up, he'd been hovering over me, the strangest expression on his face.

I'd tugged down my short skirt—thanks to Mila. "Are you trying to look up my skirt?"

"No," he'd said and straightened back up, hands raised. "I swear there was something in your hair and—"

"Sniffing my hair?"

"Fuck no."

"Then back up, please." And I'd shooed him back a few inches.

He'd smirked and grumbled something about picky artists needing their space for their big heads. I'd laughed.

Even though the tension between us was electric, our playing was incredible. His husky singing voice held secrets, and I got lost in the sound we made, my soul clicking with something in his.

Hadn't it always been that way with us?

My head kept going back to the stolen moment in the walk-in cooler at Rio.

He'd been erratic and crazy and slightly deranged. The truth was I had gotten under his skin and my gut knew it terrified him.

Now here it was Friday already, and I sat next to the pool, working on the guest list for the gala. Mrs. Smythe and I had met or spoken on the phone frequently, nailing down the details. Counting the kids and attendees, over three hundred people would be in attendance at the black tie affair at the Beverly Wilshire Hotel. A formal event, each attendee would pay two thousand dollars a plate. Thank goodness, Wilson had been over a couple of times with his list of Hollywood celebrities to invite. Since our lunch at the Rio, he'd helped me quite a bit.

I glanced up when Sebastian walked up to the patio from his property, holding a brown wicker basket with a closed lid. Strange sounds came from it.

"Hey you," he said, and leaned in to give me a quick peck on my cheek. Nothing serious, and he didn't linger.

I cocked my head. "Your basket is freaking me out."

He chuckled. "I don't buy presents for girls much, so I hope I wasn't too far off the mark with this, but I'd like you to meet fur ball—which isn't really her name. You can call her whatever you want," he said as he pulled out a fluffy, slobbering little puppy.

I blinked at it. I could barely take care of myself. "A puppy?"

He plopped her in my arms. "Duh. She's for you, goof."

She whimpered and licked my hand. "But why? What do I do with it? Where does it sleep? Does it eat cheese puffs? Oh God. I'd suck at being a parent."

He lifted his soft blue eyes to mine. "It's a stupid gift, isn't it?"

I shook my head. She *was* terribly cute with her big brown eyes and long hair. "No, no, no. Why do you say that? Wait, is this some kind of break-up-dog? Because you feel *guilty* about what happened?"

His jaw tightened. "Stop putting words in my mouth. This is because when I saw this dog, I knew she had to be yours. She's sweet . . . like you. She's musical . . . I heard her howl at the pet store. She's got the softest fur . . . just like you." He chuckled at my expression.

"Okay, not even touching the fur comment, but why were you even thinking of me?" I pressed.

He looked deflated. Shit, I was ruining this. "Why what?" he said. "Can't I just do something spontaneous? Why do you have to put a label on it?"

I sighed. "So you think about me? A lot. Like when you just randomly walk in a pet store? And not just when you go to bed and have sex dreams about me?"

"Yeah. I also think about food a lot, too."

Ha. Fine. I gazed back down at the gorgeous dog that seemed to be some kind of Yorkie.

I rubbed her head and she licked me. "Well, thank you. I'm in love with her already. I'm going to call her Tater." She yipped delicately. "She likes it."

His lips quirked. "Tater? After me?"

"No, because I like French Fries," I chuckled. "I hope she doesn't like to jump in the pool like Monster did."

175

"That was a wonderful night," he said with a wistful expression. "You and me talking until dawn. Until I left, of course."

I covered my face. "I can't believe I ran down here and just—kissed you."

He chuckled. "It was the Romeo quote that did it, wasn't it? Works every time."

I punched his arm. "I thought I was the only one you'd quoted that to."

He got a serious look on his face. "Only you, V, only you."

He sat down next to me in a lounge chair, and I looked at him harder, noticing the disheveled hair and the dark circles.

"Are you okay? You seem tired."

He didn't meet my eyes. "I'm cool. Besides the studio, Spider and I got signed for another commercial."

There was more, though. Something was on his mind.

I winced. "Any news on the Hing movie?"

He shook his head, his eyebrows gathering in. "Nah, I didn't get it. It's official. Whatever, I was a long shot with him—everyone knows that—obviously." He rose. "I'll talk you tomorrow at the studio. Take care of Tater for me."

Oh.

My heart hurt at the disappointment on his face. "I'm so sorry. They'll be other movies, other directors. Right?"

"Yeah." And then he walked away from me, and I wanted to call him back.

But we were different now. Uneasy and afraid to be alone together for too long.

It sucked.

❦

Mila had made good on her night out with Baxter. She rented us a Mercedes limo that Saturday night and made us reservations at a new club called Krush. We picked up Baxter, who was sexy gorgeous with his linebacker body and big dimples—until you noticed he only had eyes for the dudes. We didn't care. He was fun, picked up on our vibe to dance, and kept the creeps away.

We'd just finished dancing and I'd headed to the bar to get us another round when I felt a hand on my shoulder. "Quit your whining, Baxter, here's your Buttery Nipple," I called out triumphantly as I turned around drink in hand.

But it wasn't Baxter. It was Blair.

"Well, if it isn't the sweet little violinist named *Violet St. Lyons.*" Her lips curled up in a snarl.

My entire body tensed. "Blair. Nice to see you. I'm actually here with some friends—so if you'll excuse me." I made to brush by her, but she blocked me.

"Oh, don't be in such a rush. I still want to talk, *Violet.*"

Going by the slight flush on her face and the smeared makeup, she was trashed. I smiled tightly. Might as well let her get her say in. "Fine."

She shooed a girl off the stool next to her and then plopped down, crossing her tanned legs delicately at the ankles. She sipped on a glass of wine and sent me a haughty glare. Something she seemed to have mastered. "I don't know what you're doing to keep Sebastian away from me, but you need to chill out. You're ruining his career."

"He can make it without you, and I think you know that. Find a new boy toy—unless you're in love with him?" The thought had crossed my mind.

She laughed. "God, I may have had sex with him which was *fantastic*—and I may have fallen in love with him for a second or two—but romance is *not* my ultimate goal. Success and longevity in Hollywood is." She took a sip, her slitted eyes on my face. "Not that you would know about ambition. Your music career seems to have taken a nosedive rather dramatically."

That stung. "You don't know the first thing about me or my music."

She tossed her head back and chuckled. "You're quite the feisty thing, aren't you, but I think I prefer the freak from the coffee shop. At least she had the sense to run away." She ran her finger across the rim of her glass. "Let me put it like this, *Violet*: You may have skated by without anyone picking up on who you are, but I know. And for some odd reason, it bothers you for people to know. All it would take would be a mention that you were the reason Sebastian Tate left me, and people would *hate* you." She fluttered her spidery eyelashes at me. "To prevent me from spilling the beans, I think you should talk to Sebastian, convince him to amp up *our* relationship—maybe even a fake proposal." She bit her lip. "God, I'd love to try on wedding dresses and buy a ring and plan a bachelorette party."

The room spun. Being in the eye of a paparazzi storm? Terrifying. I licked my lips, feeling cold and then hot. My mouth dried and I started tapping with my free hand. I dropped the shot and the glass shattered, alcohol and glass flying. Someone screamed and people gave me a wide birth as they looked accusingly at the mess and then me, but I was frozen, fighting my panic, fighting Blair.

"Dearest, maybe you should sit down. You really *are* a basket case." She *tsked*.

No. Not this time.

From somewhere deep inside me, some small part of the girl I used to be reared her head. Yet, because of my parents, I wasn't an evil person either. And when I gazed inward I saw myself clearly. I saw that I was better. I saw that no matter what had happened to me, I at least had a chance for a future happiness. I wasn't so sure Blair did.

I stepped in so close to her I could see the pores of her skin. She definitely needed a chemical peel.

"I see who you are," I said. "You're a small-town girl with a big talent and it got you far. Look at you . . . you're America's Sweetheart, but now that you're getting older, you're mean. Ugly. Maybe I should be angry with you, but when it comes down to it, I'm not. I know what death is, Blair. I fell twenty thousand feet from the sky into a cold ocean. I watched my mother bleed to death in front of me. My father drowned so I could live. So, if you think that I am going to sit by and worry about what some jaded actress from lower Alabama has to say about spilling my secrets to the press, you're sadly wrong. You are an infinitesimal zit on this universe, and there are plenty of other issues worth my time." I gathered myself. Smiled. "Oh, and I wanted to personally thank you for your fifty thousand dollar contribution to Lyons Place. *Indie Rock Today* announced it this morning." I leaned in and gave her a squeeze. "God loves you."

I walked off on shaky legs, but with victory in my bones.

CHAPTER 18

"My favorite color is cobalt—also cornflower or indigo or azure or steel or lake or sky—hell, I just love blue."—Spider (Clarence)

"HOW MANY BLUE SHIRTS DO YOU NEED?" I ASKED SPIDER AS WE left Gucci and headed down Rodeo Drive. He might look like a thug, but he was a well-dressed one, always scouting the men's stores for the best looks and designers.

We strolled along wearing Dallas Cowboys caps pulled low and aviators. Not that it helped much. Those hardcore fans always recognized us.

"I'm in what I'm going to call my *blue phase*, whether it's my hair or that sick blue Lamborghini we looked at last week." He lit a cig and blew out smoke. "I think I'm going to buy it. What do you think?" He slid his eyes at me. "Dude, you look like shit warmed over."

"Thanks. That's just the look I was going for."

I'd agreed to come along even though all I really wanted was to go home and crash. Usually I was the Energizer Bunny. Not today. Something clawed at me. Maybe it was because I'd been up until two in the morning drinking and waiting for V to play. Same as the night before. But she never did. The only time I saw her was at the studio. I'd even tried to talk up Mrs. Smythe and find out what days she'd be at the orphanage, but the woman was tight-lipped on all things V.

She'd said she wouldn't regret us, but she did. Most of the

time, all I wanted was to just pull her in my arms and kiss her, but I couldn't lead her on.

I had nothing to offer her. No love. No future. Just friendship and sex. I rubbed my face. Since when did Sebastian Tate wallow in self-pity over a girl?

Just then I saw Blair across the street, walking with her flashy entourage in tow.

My mind went back to the day Harry had introduced me to her in his office a few months ago, before we'd moved to LA. She'd been sitting there splayed out on his leather couch like a Playboy centerfold, her shirt unbuttoned down to her waist and tiny boy shorts on. She'd giggled at me, flicked her hair over her shoulder and tackle hugged me, her melons squashed against my chest. Her body was tight, no denying it, but underneath she was a twisted bitch. Only I hadn't been able to see it at first. I'd just wanted to fuck her, plain and simple. Harry had sucked me in with his idea of making us a couple. *Be seen around town*, he'd said. *Pretend you're in a committed relationship*, he'd encourage. *The Hing movie will fall in your lap*, he'd promised. And maybe it would have worked if V hadn't came along, but I wasn't blaming her. I blamed myself. I'd willingly agreed to the lies just to get ahead. Sure other couples in Hollywood did it all the time, but I was disappointed in myself. Lying wasn't me. Hadn't I told V that I valued honesty? *I* was a fucking joke.

I grabbed Spider's arm and muscled him through the door of the next store. "Hide," I hissed. "I can't deal with her shit today."

"Who? Godzilla? Zombies?" He gazed around at the glittery displays in the store and paled. "Dude, we're in Tiffany's. If you're here to get me to buy a ring for Mila, you can just back the f—"

In a cloud of cloyingly sweet perfume, Blair waltzed through the door. She rushed up to me just as her entourage surrounded Spider. He grinned and welcomed them with open arms. *Fuck*. I just wanted to run.

"Basty, baby! I'm about to pee myself that Tiffany's is where you wanted to meet me." She smiled brilliantly and then leaned in to hiss in my ear. "Act like you're happy to see me."

I arched a brow. "I came in here to get away from you."

Her big lips tightened as she pulled me to the side. "I have called you a million times, asshole. I heard you went horseback riding—without me. I also heard you practically begged V to talk to you at Rio's."

I narrowed my eyes. Was she following me?

"So what? I didn't get the part, anyway."

Her strapless dress swelled as she sucked in a sympathetic breath. Her voice was sugary. "Harry told me. Apparently, I'm still in, but if we keep up this nonsense of not being seen—"

"Stop," I snapped. "I've been doing some soul searching and I don't care anymore about negative publicity. You can do your best. Paint me as the bad guy. Tell everyone I cheated on you. Make yourself look fucking *golden*. It doesn't matter to me. I am ending this charade. I want my life back."

Her mouth opened. "*This* is all about that little twit of a girl, isn't it?"

A roaring took up in my head. "So help me God, Blair, don't bring her name into this. She's *nothing* to do with this."

A tinkling laugh came out of her. "You're in love with her, aren't you? Some stupid girl named *Violet* who plays the *violin*. It's so incredibly ridiculous and trite that I can't even fathom what you'd see in—"

"This fake relationship is done." I gritted my teeth. "My suggestion is you get your PR girl to meet with Mila and let the two of them work out a statement together. But if you so much as touch V with scandal, I will hunt you—"

"If you think that I'm going to sit by while you ride off into the sunset with your one true love, then you have me all wrong." She fluttered her lashes and called to the girls over my shoulder. "Come along, ladies. Apparently Sebastian needs some space to pick out my engagement ring."

They flashed their camera phones at us and floated out the door.

Spider said, "Bollocks, she's scary as shit. Meaner than my Irish whiskey-drinking Grandma."

My adrenaline plummeted. I weaved and clutched the side of the jewelry counter.

"What the hell, mate?" Spider caught me by the arm. He steered me toward the hovering saleslady who'd already pulled out a rolling chair for me.

"I'm not a baby, Spider."

"You're pale and weaving like you're hammered." He leaned in to check my face. "You haven't been drinking, have you?"

Not since last night. I pushed him away. "No. Get out of my face."

"Bloody hell, you're a belligerent one."

Dizziness hit and the room twirled. "Fuck," I muttered, and leaned over to put my head between my knees. "Sorry, man. Give me a minute. I forgot to eat this morning, that's all." Truth. In fact, I'd lost a few pounds since the camping trip two weeks before.

He hovered around me. "Normally I'd avoid talking about your personal life—too touchy feely for me—but you're in the shitter, my friend. You're distracted half the time, not eating, staying up late and generally in a pissy mood twenty-four seven.

Is it because you didn't get the movie or is it because you slept with V and now you regret it?"

"Fuck you," I muttered, and sat back up in the chair. "I need something to eat, that's all."

He turned back to the saleslady who'd moved to stand behind the jewelry counter. "Excuse me? Do you have some candy here or maybe a power bar?"

He focused back on me and let out a sigh. "Okay, here's what I think: You came to Hollywood to settle down . . . for roots . . . V *is* your roots, man."

I shook my head. "I can't even look at her without wanting—fuck, I don't know—more. But all I can think of is Emma's lies. Not so much Emma herself, because I'm over her—but still, she lied to me and V lied to me. And then there's Geoff. I keep thinking she's going to up and run back to him. Go back to New York. Especially now that her music is back."

"Dude, you're the glue that holds us all together. *You.* We all gravitate toward you. Me, Mila, your fans, even Blair. V is no different. Give her a chance."

The saleslady pushed a power bar in my hands and I tore it open and inhaled it.

I *was* losing it, and I knew why.

I didn't want to be without V in my life.

Her music had sucked me in from the beginning, wedging into my bones, but it hadn't been until the night at the canyon that my heart had connected the dots. We'd been extraordinary. And it wasn't just the sex. I got her; I saw straight through her grief to the beautiful part of her that was aching to emerge. Her darkness had called to me, her music had enthralled me, but it was her soul that was mine.

Was that love?

It was midnight and V still wasn't home.

She'd yet to return from her night out with Mila. I'd called her earlier to see if we could watch a movie, and maybe I'd be able to talk to her, but she'd already had plans—which is how I found myself dog-sitting for Tater at her house. Spider had dog-sat the last time they'd gone out. He hadn't been happy about it either, us at home while they partied at the clubs.

I sat out on her patio lounge chair while Tater slept on my chest.

My phone pinged. Mila kept sending me texts and photos of them out at some club. Pics of V chugging tequila. Pics of her twerking with some beefy looking dude. I was getting angry.

Half an hour later, I heard a car pull up, so I stood and walked around to the front of the house, still holding Tater. She climbed out of her car looking dangerously sexy in a red mini skirt and heels. I bit back a snarl imagining male hands on her tonight.

"Aw, she's asleep," she said as she leaned over to peer at Tater's face. "Thank you for watching her."

"Did you have a good time?" My voice was laced with tightness.

Did she really love me or had she just said those words in the moment?

She nodded. "Yes, and I'm sorry if Mila kept texting you. She had this hare-brained idea of infuriating you and Spider into . . ."

Silence settled between us as her voice trailed off.

"What?" I snapped.

"Nothing," she sighed. "Thank you for keeping Tater.

Do—do you want to come inside or go sit on the patio?"

"Patio," I said and we walked around the house and came to a stop at a table next to the pool. I sat Tater down on a seat cushion. "Look, V, there's something I need to say." I swallowed.

She got still, her eyes searching my face. "Yeah?"

I paced around. "Something's wrong with me. I can't write, play music, act, sleep. *Eat.* All I do is think about you."

Her face softened. "Oh."

My stomach fluttered with nerves. "I don't care what anyone thinks, but I need you in my life everyday. I don't want to wake up and not see you in my bed, V." I leaned down to her and pushed both hands in her hair and tugged her to me. "Please give me a chance, V."

"What about Blair? Your career?"

"I want the world to know you're mine. I ended things with Blair."

She looked away from me, making me antsy. Doubt niggled at me.

"I won't stand for you messing with Geoff, V. Tell me now if you want him back."

"No, it isn't that. It's Blair. She came up to me at the club earlier this week. It's never going to be over for her."

I kissed her softly. "Focus on us. Give us a chance, and I mean more than just a one night stand."

She nodded and her eyes searched mine, as if waiting for something more.

"What?"

She swallowed and looked away. "It's just—you know how I feel."

She wanted me to say *I love you.*

CHAPTER 19

"Love. Once I'd pushed it away. Now, I'd die without it."
—from the journal of Violet St. Lyons

I LOVED HIM. THESE PAST WEEKS WITHOUT HIM HAD BEEN TORTURE.

Did that mean I was willing to accept us when he didn't feel the same way?

Maybe.

He caressed my face. "We can sit out here all night and talk, but I'm dying to sink into you. You owe me, you know," he said huskily.

"Why?"

"Because I'm going to make you pay for dancing with those guys," he said as he stripped off my slinky shirt, easing the fabric off and tossing it on the ground. He kissed my neck and then nibbled gently on my ear. "I keep picturing you in that swing with your legs spread for me."

I moaned. "Me, too."

"Strip for me, V." He took a step back from me, a need so visceral in his gaze that I shivered.

"Out here on the patio? Do you have something against bedrooms?"

"It's where we started," he said.

I unzipped my skirt and stood before him in nothing but my heels.

His face reddened. "What the fuck? No bra and no panties

187

tonight?" His hands clenched.

I bit my lip. "I took the panties off when I pulled up to the house."

"Oh, you're a naughty girl." He sat back on a chair, eyes at half-mast, a smoldering expression on his face. "I want you to play for me just like that, V. I want to see your body when you let go with music."

Need knifed through me. "What do you want me to play?"

"Play how you feel about me," he said softly. "I took the liberty of getting your violin for you already. It's on the table."

I cocked an eyebrow. "You had this planned?"

"No, I just wanted to hear you play, but this is even better." He bit his lower lip and groaned, watching me as I sashayed over to the violin. I made a show of it, leaning over the table to pick it up and placing it in the crook of my neck. I don't know if it looked sexy or not, but he seemed to like it.

I took a deep breath.

How could I choose the song that conveyed the depth of how I felt? That I felt like we'd known each other our entire lives even though it had only been a short time?

In the end, I went with "Truly Madly Deeply" by Savage Garden.

I poured my heart into my sound, and when his voice chimed in on the chorus, I adjusted to his cadence. I closed my eyes when his hands cupped my breasts, his mouth not far behind. I raised my elbows to give him room, and my music faltered.

"Don't stop," he whispered in my ear. "I want you while you break free."

I played on, stretching into the melody, drawing out the low notes as they reverberated between us. My body was under his spell, and I let it all go, my head going back, embracing us. For so long I'd believed that the price of love was too high, but now, with him, I saw a glimmer of the future, of us playing music, laughing, loving.

"Incandescent," he murmured, and fell to his knees, his hands on my waist. He nudged my legs apart, his fingers skimming my wet core like little brushes of electricity. I shivered.

"Sebastian," I groaned as his tongue snaked in and found my clit. I abruptly stopped playing.

"Need you now, V," he growled, his voice rough.

I set my violin down even as he tugged his shirt over his head. His pants and underwear and shoes were next. I took in his tall frame, the toned biceps, the cut abs—the big cock. I pulled him to me and kissed him hard, my tongue tangling with his.

"You going all alpha on me? I like it," he chuckled.

I laughed and we kissed, his hands molding to my ass, sliding me against him. He groaned and pulled back, breathing heavily, his forehead pressed against mine.

"What's wrong?" I asked.

"It's just, the *feels* for you are so intense, so crazy, it's got me worked up and I wanna say all this stuff and do all these erotic things to you—dirty things—and then I want to worship you, too. That night on the swing, I was rough." He swallowed. "I'm just trying to reel myself back a notch or two."

"Are you kidding me? I like you like that. *I need it.* It reminds me that I'm alive, Sebastian."

He leaned into me. "V, I l—"

"What is it?"

He took a deep breath. "I—I need you. Now."

And then his mouth hit mine and thinking was over. We

collapsed down on a patio lounge chair, and I straddled him, working his thickness inside me.

He cupped my face and showed me how he felt without words, by kissing me like he needed me to breathe. He showed me love in his own way, and we went there together, over the edge.

CHAPTER 20

"My life had followed a strict plan for five years. Until V."
—Sebastian Tate

AROUND THREE IN THE MORNING, WE COLLAPSED IN V'S BED while Tater rested in her basket next to us, grunting and snoring. V did her own fair share of snoring, her body curled into mine. To be honest, I'd have slept much better in my own damn bed, but when it came to V, sleep was not on my list of priorities.

I couldn't seem to close my eyes anyway, too keyed up about us. I had to figure out a way to get her used to the press, because they would be after us. Sure, we could stay inside all the time, but I didn't want a life like that.

The sun peeked in through the window, illuminating her face. She looked like a rock and roll angel, her purple hair spilling out over my arm, long lashes resting on pale cheeks. I curved my hand around her hip and inhaled her scent. Rightness filled me. *This.* And for a moment I got a glimpse of what our future might be, countless mornings of us waking up together, nights wrapped in each other's arms.

She stretched her luscious body and then turned to me, eyes sleepy.

I smoothed the hair out of her face. "I don't know who snored louder, you or Tater."

"Ladies don't snore."

"My love, you are no lady. Not after the things we did last night."

"Oh, yeah?" She bit her full lips. "Then what am I? A groupie who bagged the lead singer?"

I kissed my way up her neck, paying special attention to her collarbone. "All you got to know is this . . . *you're mine*," I growled, lifting her leg over my hip, positioning myself to take her. Own her.

I pushed the word *love* out of my head.

⁂

I cooked V breakfast in her huge kitchen while she told me about her parents.

"I didn't have a normal childhood. I mean, yeah, we were rich, but they didn't focus on that. So when I moved out here, it was to run away, but in the back of my mind, I was planning the orphanage as a way to honor them. To show them that I could carry on their work in a small way."

I planted a kiss on her lips. I loved how she thought of others. "I still get goosebumps when I think that we might have been at the orphanage at the same time."

"Yeah. I met this great kid there. Kevin. You need to play for him. I can tell he's special."

She smiled as I slid a cheese omelet to her. I even went to her pantry, found her cheese puffs and sprinkled some on the side. "You can have some of these, but now that I'm here, you need to start eating better."

She rolled her eyes, but didn't give me grief. Her mouth was already stuffed with food.

Spider and Mila showed up at the back door, and I ended

up cooking for the entire crew. Even Tater got a piece of bacon.

Spider watched me quizzically as he nibbled on a piece of toast. "What I can't understand is why you bought her a dog. Isn't Monster enough of a handful?"

"Practically an engagement ring from a fecking Tate man," Mila chimed in.

I laughed nervously and glanced at Mila, and maybe it was the ring statement that got to me, but mostly I noticed that Mila didn't look like herself. Her normal cheerful banter seemed faked and her headband slightly askew. It worried me.

And the day went downhill from there.

Later that morning, I was on my way out the door, back to V's after my shower, when a messenger dropped off a package from Blair. I stared down at the brown manila envelope.

A script? A love letter? Not likely.

I tore the envelope open and what was there made my heart bang in my chest.

Photos of me and V—photos of me and Blair.

With growing horror, I flipped through pictures obviously taken last night of V playing for me in the nude and us making love. Lastly, there were pictures of me and Blair in my bed— selfie style—taken by Blair as was obvious from the angle from which she'd held her cell phone. The tops of her boobs were visible, and I appeared asleep, my head turned to the side on the pillow.

I pulled out my phone and checked to see if I'd even drunk dialed her that night.

No record of it.

Feeling like I might pass out, I sat down.

A note was taped to one of the selfies.

Basty Boy,

You can't leave me in the dust and not expect retaliation. America is going to feel so sad for me when they see what a cheater you are. Good luck with the backlash, asshole.

Smooches, Blair xoxo

I jerked up and called her and got nada but her voicemail.

Bitch! I called again. And again, working myself up to a fever pitch until my head pounded.

Finally, I called Harry's office to talk to him—anybody—but his secretary said he was out of the office. I lost it. I told her to tell him that his ass was fired. If I could manage my own band, I sure as hell could find my own damn movies.

V.

Had to warn her of the shitstorm that was coming.

I gathered the photos up, my fingers hesitating over the ones of Blair and me. *Fuck!* I dreaded V seeing me with her, but it had to be done. I tucked them under my arm and went to her house. When she didn't answer the front door, I eased around to the back and went in through the patio, calling her name.

Nothing but silence. Weird.

Hearing the soft rumble of her voice through her bedroom door, I tapped lightly and entered. I found her sitting on her bed. Her head was dripping wet and a towel was wrapped around her. Whoever called her had been important enough to pull her out of the shower.

"I need to talk to you," I said, my voice tight.

She nodded and held her hand up to indicate "just a minute."

I exhaled heavily.

"Okay," she said to the person on the line, putting her back to me as she fished around in her dresser for clothes. She stood and slipped on a pair or red lacy underwear and a tank. "Look, I need to go now. Someone's here."

A pause. "Yes, it's him. We're together."

I froze. *Geoff.*

"Thank you . . ." she said, her voice lower now as she walked out onto her balcony.

"V, get off the phone." My hands were clenched now, and it wasn't about the pictures so much as *him.* I didn't like how soft her voice was . . . secretive.

She paused mid-sentence but then kept talking, her finger telling me to wait a minute.

I counted the seconds. Seventy-two. I was livid.

She said goodbye and came back in the room.

"Who was that?" I growled.

"Geoff, and before you go caveman on me, *you're* the one I want to be with. Not him. He knows about us."

Still hurt to hear her say his fucking name.

"I don't want you talking to him."

She reared back. "He's my friend, the only link I have left to my parents."

"He's still in love with you," I retorted.

Her brows came together. "Don't jump to conclusions just because he called. You can trust me."

Heat flushed over me. "We're together, V. I'm not with anyone else. And if I even suspect you still have feelings—"

She stormed out of the room, headed downstairs.

"Wait," I called, following her. "Don't walk out on me."

She didn't stop, her shoulders stiff when she finally faced me in the den as I walked over to make sure the blinds were closed. I didn't want any more photos taken of us.

I tried to rein in my anger. I was irrational when it came to her and Geoff, but it wasn't something I could control easily. "Talk to me about Geoff. Explain."

"He called to tell me that he'd turned in my application to the Manhattan School of Music."

My whole damn world came to a standstill.

Of course she wanted to go back to school. She was getting her life together, figuring out what she wanted.

"You're leaving?" My tone was incredulous.

"What if I did?" she snapped. "Would you really care? What we're doing is fun, but we don't have a commitment. You have your life here, and soon you'll be on the road or going to a movie set."

I found I needed air. I sucked in a sharp breath and blew it out. That didn't help, so I sat down. "What matters is *he* will be near you and I won't. You have a history with him. Do you think I like imagining you hanging out with him? Rekindling your friendship until it turns into something else? Maybe you get tired of me working on the road, and he's there, so you find yourself spending more and more time with him? Why can't you go to school somewhere here in California?"

She groaned. "Why can't you trust me?"

I jerked up. "I want you *here* with me. I want you beside me, under me, in my bed, and so far up in my business that I can't fucking move for bumping into you." My hands fisted, pushing out my next words. I met her gaze, the old festering wound that was at the center of my heart rising up. "If you go to New York, we're over."

Silence.

Fuck! Why had I said that?

"Shit, don't leave me, V. Not-not when I just found you."

She shook her head. "What does it matter? You'll find another girl."

Her words cut me, and I looked down at the photos. This would ensure she'd leave me.

"We have worse problems, V. Blair's got photos of us."

CHAPTER 21

*"Then he came along, and like a twisted piece of metal that's burned
beyond recognition, I emerged from the fire. Different. Changed."*
—from the journal of Violet St. Lyons

MY FRAGILE WORLD WAS COLLAPSING.
I sipped on tequila that he'd poured me and looked down at the pictures again. He'd downed two shots of bourbon already, his hands unsteady.

Pics of me. Of us. *Of her.*

"These will be in the papers and on every social media site she can get to post them," he said. "You are all I'm worried about, V."

I gazed at them, my eyes stopping over one of us on my patio, him on his knees with his mouth between my legs as my body arched in ecstasy. My skin blazed at the memory, echoes of the passion we'd shared—and now everyone in the world would see. The society people in New York. Geoff. My old musician friends. Worst of all, the board of directors for the orphanage.

My stomach dropped when I saw the ones of him and Blair, her lips stuck out in that stupid duck face. Frozen, I stared at it. Unable to focus on anything but his face on a pillow next to hers.

My eyes flashed from one picture to the next, and I bent over to breathe better.

Inhale and exhale. Don't vomit.

"I know what you're thinking, but the one of Blair—it happened the night I came over here and Geoff was here. She showed up at my house when I was trashed and got in my bed. She must have thought I'd fuck her if she was there. Nothing happened. I woke up and she was just there. That's the morning you saw her leaving my house."

I swallowed. "*Something* happened. Her boobs are on your chest."

He kneeled down. "V, I had no clue she was even in my bed until I woke up. You were the only thing I could think about that night. You and Geoff."

I turned my head away from him and clutched my glass as if it were a lifeline, realizing the magnitude. The Mystery Girl and Sebastian Tate would finally be splayed out for millions to post, share, tweet, and crucify. Someone would probably write a song about it. It would definitely be fodder for the comedians on SNL.

I looked down at the pictures. "Remind me to pass on the makeup next time. And to not have sex outdoors. Obviously," I said, forcing my shoulders to move in a nonchalant shrug like I didn't care, but he knew the truth. I was devastated by these.

"If I can talk to her, maybe I can convince her not to go through with it. I'm so fucking sorry."

I was barely listening.

She'd won. At everything. Because even if she didn't have him, she'd have public sympathy and a career. I had nothing. Not even him. Not really.

He was willing to toss us away just because I suggested I might want to go back to New York. Of course, I'd never leave him if he wanted me with him. I could do music anywhere.

If he could tell me he loved me.

He said my name in that husky voice of his, the one that sounded like sex, the one that made me want to rip his clothes off. "Violet—"

"Stop," I said, clenching my fists. I stood and faced him, tossing back the last of my shot. "First off, I wish we'd never met." I held my hand up. "No. Wait. I don't wish that because then I wouldn't know Spider or Mila. I—I wish I'd *never* fallen for you. Loving means losing, just like my parents." I sucked in a breath.

He closed his eyes, a dazed expression on his face as if my words crushed him.

"You make me wish for things that will never be," I whispered. "You want to be a star, and all I want is *you*."

He scrubbed his face. "V, I'm sorry I got you involved with her. I'm going to do what I can to keep it out of the papers."

"What? Go running back to her? Just to save me from public humiliation? What about your own reputation? How will Nora and Leo react to seeing their baby brother all over the media in the nude?"

More panic settled in me. Stares. Whispers. People who wanted to delve into my box of grief. "She couldn't have timed this better. I'll have to cancel the benefit. I can't face those people. *I can't.*"

I wasn't strong enough.

He'd stopped his pacing, a muscle jerking in his cheek as he leaned down until his nose was level with mine. "Then this is goodbye, Violet? You're giving up on us already?"

Did I hear a break in his voice? *Impossible.*

"If I don't say goodbye, then you will." I walked past him, enjoying the hiss of breath when I let my hand drift over his crotch. "This moment is begging for a soundtrack, don't you think?" I said, coming to a stop by the stereo system and cranking up Kurt Cobain's "Smells Like Teen Spirit." Holding my hands up in the "horns rocking out" signal, I bobbed my head to the beat while he watched, anger flickering across his face. I danced and twirled around, closing my eyes, the music vibrating through my body, my fingers itching for my violin.

My eyes flew open. He'd strode over to me and clicked the stereo off, chest *still* heaving. He shoved his hands in my hair and dragged my face to his, and I groaned at the fire that blazed in my body. I felt the warm heat of his skin, and I pressed closer and inhaled. He smelled like bourbon and sex—a rock star's diet—and I panted with need, cursing myself at the same time.

How would I ever get over him?

He pressed his thumbs across my mouth. Gentle. But his voice was angry. "You can't wait to high-tail it back to your lawyer boyfriend, can you?"

"I plead the fifth," I ground out, staring at his full lips. I licked my own.

We stared at each other until he exhaled heavily and put his back to me, his muscles as taut as the guitar strings he played. He verged on breaking.

Yeah, well, welcome to my world. For two years I'd been a prisoner of pain, and I'd be damned before I let him put me back there.

Yet at the same time, I reached my hand out to him. Stupid hand.

But of course, he didn't see it.

"So long, V," he said soft as a whisper, staring at the ground as if *I* was breaking *his* heart, when all along it was the other way around.

My lungs seized and words failed me.

Just look at me! I wanted to scream as his broad shoulders faced his house as if ready to leave. In truth, it wasn't me who was giving up, but him. I was merely pushing him toward the choice I already knew he wanted.

It happened. He took a step from me, then another and another until he was nothing but a speck as he crossed the grass between our houses.

I clutched my chest and wanted to fall to the ground and rail on it. Alone. *Again.*

&

The rest of the morning passed in a blur. I drank more tequila and ended up on the couch. My phone buzzed on and off. I didn't care, my head replaying pictures of me nude, pictures of Blair and Sebastian.

I refused to cry over him.

Mila came and banged on my door. I ignored her.

Wilson called and left me several voicemails.

Geoff called again, but I never picked up. Nothing mattered.

Mrs. Smythe called, and I immediately felt sick. How could I tell her that me as the public figure of the orphanage was in danger.

Should I step down as the spokesperson?

Should I give up on my dreams?

Where was the resolve and guts-over-fear attitude I'd adopted?

Where was Violet?

I walked around the house, running my fingers over things that belonged to my parents. A photo of us on vacation in Paris that sat on a table in the den, a scarf my mother knitted for me one Christmas that hung on a peg, my father's astronomy journal next to mine on the coffee table. With a deep breath, I opened it and traced his slanted handwriting. I flipped to the last entry, made a few weeks before his death. Emotion clawed at my chest as I read it . . . as I had a million times before.

"Saw a meteor shower tonight and it reminded me of Violet. Bright. Full of hope. We wait with bated breath to see how she shines."

I set the book down.

And at the end of it all, I reminded myself that I'd survived that horrific day.

I'd LIVED.

I was a fighter, and I was going to fight.

◌

After lunch, I went to Wilson's after listening to his rather frantic messages about needing to talk to me. He also kept apologizing, but I couldn't for the life of me think why.

He opened the door, wearing his LA Lakers hat, and led me to his office where I got a jolt.

Oh.

Dan Hing sat in a black leather chair, nursing a drink. I knew Wilson had powerful connections, but this was odd.

"I guess I should have called. Want me to come back later?" I commented.

Wilson shifted from one foot to the other, a cagey look on his face. "Truth is I wanted to talk to you alone, but since you're here . . ."

What was going on? I flicked my eyes at Hing, seeing an opportunity, but just not sure how to play it. Maybe I could salvage some of this colossal mess created by Blair. So far my name wasn't popping up anywhere on the internet, so whatever she was planning, she was taking her time and making us sweat.

I sat down across from Hing, tension radiating in the room. I wasn't sure why.

Weird undercurrent or not, he was fascinating to chat with. Thirty-five years old and he'd already directed and co-produced two Academy Award-winning movies, one an independent film and the other a blockbuster World War II film. No wonder Sebastian was itching to work for him. He was movie gold.

Hipster handsome with his skinny jeans and Einstein shirt, he kept sneaking little glances at me when he thought I wasn't looking. He adjusted his black-rimmed glasses and peered at me with eagle eyes.

He didn't miss much, and I don't think he cared that I was aware he was staring.

"You seem to have something on your mind, Mr. Hing." I was feeling blunt. Bruised.

He lit a cigar. "Forgive me. It—it's just that Wilson here told me *who* you are, the lone survivor of Flight 215. I find it morbidly fascinating."

My familiar walls shot up. "I'm not a freak."

"No! Not at all." He shook his head. "You're gorgeous."

Uh-huh. I narrowed my eyes at him. He wasn't fooling me.

"I've had a shitty day, so if you have something to say, just say it."

He tossed his head back and laughed, a deep rich sound. "I like your style, V, and the way you look. The hair is a bit much for me, but it suits you—and LA. The truth is, I'm looking for a new project to develop, this time as a full producer, so I'd have complete control over it from creation to the end."

Not sure what this had to do with me.

"I've got thousands of scripts and novels on my desk. Five were bestsellers last year, but not one of them interests me. I want fresh. Something that's never been done. Something that will tug at every heartstring in America, rip their guts out and make them cry like fucking babies."

I barked out a laugh. "Want to put *me* in a movie? Sorry to disappoint, but I can't act my way out of a paper bag. At my school Christmas play they gave me the only silent part, the kid who held the star up over baby Jesus."

"That's not what I had in mind actually."

I slanted a look at Wilson, who gave me an apologetic shrug. I waited. It came.

Hing said, "Wilson mentioned—"

"Nope, leave my name out," Wilson interjected. "I told you she was a private person." He patted my hand. "Sorry, I ever brought your name up to him, sweetheart. It all started when I invited him to the benefit and before I knew it, he'd pieced together who you were. He's a one-track kind of guy and once he gets an idea—I'm sorry. I had no idea he was going to broach the topic here. I wanted to talk to you first." He sent Hing a glare.

Hing chuckled. "I made him millions on the last movie I did, V. He felt like he owed it to me to tell me about you once I inquired. I'm an asshole, but I think we have the possibility of a fantastic movie here. With you."

I felt my face redden at the discerning way he looked at me. I took to tapping my leg.

"I'm sorry," Wilson said again, his face obviously pained as he sat across from me. "If you want to go now, I wouldn't blame you."

I sucked up some nerve. I had to see this through. "No, I'm good." I turned to Hing. "You don't want me to act for you. So what were you thinking?"

He sat there for a few beats, pursing his lips. "I want your story about the crash, your battle to escape the plane, your struggles with your grief, and even the orphanage. Of course, I'd like to take a peek at your journal as well, see if we can pull anything from it."

Oh. My eyes widened. But how—

"I saw it lots of times at your house, V, but I swear I never read it or even touched it." Wilson grimaced. "You know I have my own grief with my wife. I'd never betray that."

"Don't blame Wilson. He let it slip about the journal, and once he did, I convinced him you wouldn't care if I approached you. And, if you say no, then there's no harm, no foul. We can forget we even spoke, and I'll write you a check for ten thousand dollars today for your orphanage. Either way." He paused. "I am not here to ambush you, and in fact, I had no idea you were coming over. I was here to convince Wilson to let me call you up. He was refusing, of course."

Wilson grunted. "Like you'd listen."

I waved him on with my hands. "Fine. Make your spiel to me. You're not the only Hollywood person who's ever tried to make a deal with me."

His eyes gleamed. "But you've never talked to anyone as big as me."

What was up with the level of male cockiness in this town?

"First off, I want to make this film about hope and music—I know that's important to you. I want to focus on how you grew up in this idyllic setting—Park Avenue apartments and a beach house at the Hamptons—but you lost something vital when your parents were killed . . ." and so he talked, and I listened.

He promised me millions.

"I don't need your millions, Hing. I have my own."

He pondered me. "But what if I told you that I would make you a permanent fixture on my set. You'd be able to see it in production. We could talk about your concerns."

I smiled coolly. "Hypothetically, *if* I sold it to you, I'd want more control."

He smirked and took a swig from a drink Wilson had poured him. "You're tougher than you look, V. First, I'd have to read your story to even know that if it had what I wanted."

"Don't get coy now, Hing."

He sucked on his cigar.

I shifted around in my seat, getting comfortable. I took my time as I eyed him, sipping on a glass of water. I set it down. "Do you know how terrifying it was to see people sucked out of a plane? And for some reason people want details." I got lightheaded talking about it, but it wasn't as bad as in the past. I had to do this. Face my fears. A sense of calm came over me. "Did you know that nightmares have haunted me for two years, and it wasn't until recently that I pieced together that my father actually saved me? Now, I can recall him fighting to get me on that seat cushion. He put me there, and then let go. So I could live."

Hing's mouth parted.

I continued. "I'm sure you've seen the pictures of them hauling me up in the harness to that helicopter, but what you may not know is technically I had no heartbeat nor was I breathing. The medic brought me back with CPR. Wouldn't you like to know what I saw when I was *dead*?" I said softly.

His hand stilled its tapping against the desk.

"If you want my story, then give me what I want." I had no idea what I wanted. Not yet.

He nodded. "Fine, I'll make you an associate producer. You

can be there from day one. You will have a vote in wardrobe, talent, location, hell even the damn gripper boy. Does that make you happy?"

I kept my face blank.

"Think on it, V." He grinned. "Now that we have that out of the way, let's talk about Sebastian Tate."

My mouth flew open and my eyes went straight to Wilson. *Could he not keep any of my secrets?*

He held his hands up. "I have no idea what he's talking about. Swear."

"What?" Hing said. "Does this mean you and him are—a thing? All I meant is that he's your neighbor and I was wondering if you knew him. I was under the impression he was dating Blair Storm? Am I wrong?"

"It's not what you think," I said hurriedly.

Hing's eyes gleamed. "You're the Mystery Girl from the *Hollywood Insider*, aren't you? The one he was caught kissing."

"No."

He settled back in his chair. "I don't believe you. Is he dating Blair Storm or not? If we're going to work together, we need full disclosure, V."

"I never said we were working together, Hing."

He smiled. "Touché."

I focused on staying cool. This was Sebastian's movie career here. "I know that you didn't choose him for your zombie movie."

"True. When the story broke about him and you, I assumed there was truth to all the rumors that he was irresponsible. Plus, if I went with Blair, I wouldn't want any lover's tiffs." He tapped his ashes. "What do you know about him?"

"He's worth a million Blair Storms."

"Go on, I'm listening."

I sat there, mulling, searching for the right words. "His parents were murdered when he was eight, and even though he could have let that define him, he didn't. He's the strongest person I know, and he believes that life is *good*. His grief never broke him like it did me." I looked at my twitching hands. "He left home at eighteen, forged his own way and has managed his band ever since. He moved here for two reasons: to make a movie with you and get his friend and bandmate Spider off the road for a while. Spider *is* irresponsible and maybe even an alcoholic, but Sebastian is determined to take care of him. Sebastian's a lot like you. He sees what he wants and he goes and gets it any way he can. Not many twenty-three-year-olds can claim that."

"I see."

I shook my head. "No, you don't. *He does whatever it takes.* And maybe that means dating a starlet who promised him if he did, she'd get the part for him."

A smile worked his lips. "I'm never surprised by the things people in Hollywood will do to get what they want. I'm just as guilty as the next person. But, I guess you haven't heard yet since it was just announced by the movie company, but I went in another direction with my movie. Blair Storm did *not* get the movie. The producers wanted younger."

My body tingled in fear. "Does she know?" The loss would make Blair even crazier.

He nodded. "Yes, and Sebastian was a close contender— excellent screen test—but to be honest, I don't like rock stars-turned-actors no matter who they date. Never have. They're unpredictable."

I stood, anger flaring. "He's more than a stereotype. He's the happiest person I know—or he was until I fell in love with him. He made me realize I don't have to lose music along with everything else. I'm a fighter too, and we found each other. He's always going to be the guy who rides up on a white horse to save the girl—or a dog. He has the heart of a giver."

He smiled broadly and adjusted his glasses. "Damn, I like you, V. When you speak, all I can think is what a great line that would make in a movie."

"If I ever sell my words, it will be to someone who doesn't jump to conclusions about a person just because they're a musician. *I'm* a musician, Mr. Hing. And my whole story . . . it's still unwritten. As Sebastian once told me, I have a long way to go before I'm done."

His face softened into an understanding smile. The first genuine one. "I see. You have values—which I also like." He paused. "Maybe we can learn from each other, V."

I nodded and left.

But somehow I didn't think the conversation with Hing was entirely over.

CHAPTER 22

"We were over before we even began."—Sebastian Tate

I PACED AROUND ON MY PATIO, BINOCULARS IN HAND AS I WATCHED V get in her Maserati and drive off, seemingly headed to Wilson's since the exit for the neighborhood was in the opposite direction.

I shoved them away from me when she was out of sight and reached for my glass of bourbon. Fuck.

She'd pushed me away.

Did I blame her?

Hell, I'd walked away.

I'd let her down by letting Blair get this far. Maybe I should have been easier with Blair at the jewelry store. I'd seen how crazy she was getting, but really my head had been too caught up in V and our relationship.

How was I going to save her?

I had to stop these pictures from ever seeing the light of day.

I'd left V's earlier and driven to Blair's house and beat on the door. I'd called her and left voicemails, some angry and then toward the end I was bargaining with her, promising her that I'd serve myself up to her on a silver platter if only she'd call off the photos. God, I was willing to do anything to get her to see reason.

I was desperate, willing to compromise with a selfish lunatic.

Because of V.

I was scared of the way I felt about her. Scared that I couldn't exist in a world without her.

She was everything I wanted.

Everything I needed.

Everything.

I got weak in the legs and sat. This was not a normal reaction to a girl dumping my ass. No, this was more, and I could finally own up to what had been plain as day to me for days yet I'd refused to say it.

Our souls were one. They always had been and never in a million years would I find another girl like V. *I loved her.*

Down on my knees, wanting to beg her to take me back, I loved her.

I'd been deluding myself, focusing on my lust, but we were so much more.

I wanted to hold her in my arms and watch her sleep. I wanted to run my fingers through her hair when I kissed her. I wanted to rock her when her grief made her weep. I wanted to sleep with her body curled into mine. God. I wanted to have babies with her. I wanted to grow old with her.

Nothing mattered but V.

Not money or power.

Not being the star of the next blockbuster or recording a number one song.

Not even world peace.

Because the only thing that makes a difference in our lives is love. My parents had it. Leo had it. Violet. Love. *Us.*

CHAPTER 23

"People will stare. Make it worth the look."
—from the journal of Violet St. Lyons

THE NEXT DAY WAS THE GALA, AND MY TIME WAS RUNNING OUT.
One thing for sure, though, Blair Storm's ass was mine, and I knew exactly how to make her pay.

I got her address and phone number from Mila and at six in the morning I walked up to her door.

The day before had been insane. After meeting Hing at Wilson's, I'd driven around LA, trying to get my head straight and figure out how to use Hing's offer to my advantage. Wilson's son Mark had popped in my head, and on a whim I'd called him, explaining what I needed without divulging the details of Blair and the pictures. He'd immediately offered up one of his top entertainment lawyers at my disposal. He was sweet on me, and I'm ashamed to say I used it. The lawyer and I met Hing at the Rio, and after three hours of negotiation, we worked out a deal that was foolproof—if Blair cooperated.

Bang, bang, bang!

I knocked and yelled for ten minutes before Blair finally showed up, eyes red and swollen from crying. From losing the movie? Part of me—the side that had lived with my own loss—felt for her. My music and my parents had been all I had. Maybe acting was all she had.

She found her bitchy side and curled her lip, her narrowed

eyes glittering down at my tapping hands. "What are you doing here this early, freak?"

"You'll be thanking me later. I just saved your ass." I smiled even though my stomach was in knots.

"I don't even know what that means." She sniffed, turning her attention to her nails.

"And you won't until you invite me in. Or you tell me to go away, but you'll regret it."

She snorted and flicked a piece of flaxen hair over her shoulder. "I'm the one with photos of *you*. It was quite a hardship taking those—the bushes and wet grass wreaked havoc on my shoes. I just wish I could have been there to see your face when you looked at them."

Keep smiling, I told myself. I chuckled knowingly. "Oh, Blair, you ruined a perfectly good pair, then, because I loved those pics—except the fake ones of you, of course. They really showed your age."

She narrowed her eyes. "What do you want?"

I sighed, studying my own nails. Two can play her game. "Just a little tip: There's more to me that you think. If you'd done your research, you'd know that I have enough money to sink you in every way I can imagine, legal or not."

"Are you threatening me?" she gasped and clutched her chest.

Oh, please. "Not only can I make sure your name is smeared in every *reputable* newspaper in America, my clout in Hollywood is on the rise. I met with Hing last night. He's listening to me." I winked. "He finds me quite entertaining. I think we may be new best friends."

"How?" Her body stiffened.

"We need to chat. I suggest we move this inside. We have a

lot to discuss."

She tightened her robe and moved to the side as I entered and followed her through her spacious house. Cold and modern, it was stocked with photos of her everywhere. She led me back to the kitchen and indicated I take a seat. I stood. She did as well.

I crossed my arms. "I'll be brief. You have some pictures that belong to me, and I want them back, including the ones of you and Sebastian. I'd like the camera, your cell phone, your laptop, and any other drives where you might have downloaded the pics. I'm assuming you haven't sold them yet?"

"Not yet, but I have plans." She went to the cabinets and pulled out a can of coffee.

Keep going. Push her. "You know, it's simple really. I lost my parents, but I refuse to lose Sebastian. I will fight you every step of the way. I will destroy you to save him."

"You're boring me, Violet."

I chuckled. "Last night, I made a list of ways to ruin your life, Blair. It took up five pages in my journal." It was only one.

She planted herself in a kitchen chair and stared at me. "That's intriguing, and yet, very unlike you. How?"

"I don't tell my secrets, Blair, but if you're smart, you'll think about those pictures and the ramifications. Releasing them would be completely unpredictable. It's career suicide for *you*— not just Sebastian—although lots of people get crazy famous when sex videos of them are released. But you have no control over which way it will go."

Her eyes hardened. "What do I have to lose? At least I can get in the papers. Get sympathy."

I shook my head. "Fans are fickle. Some may rally to your side, others may listen to me, because if you do this, I *will* have my say in the media."

"So you keep saying, but I don't buy it."

I smiled tightly. "I hate to brag, but in New York my family had important friends. Even the President of the United States had dinner with my parents once, and don't think I won't call on every single contact I have to ruin you. I will go on every entertainment show in TV-land and tell them exactly how awful you are. I'll tell the police you stalked me and took those pictures to harass me. I'll hire lawyers to sue you. I might even buy your hometown in Alabama and rename it Blair Sucks—I am an heiress, after all. I will find every girl you've ever slighted or guy you've scorned and invite them to join me—"

She sent me a calculating look. "You hate attention."

"I'm running out of time and patience with you. I have a gala to attend. Give me the pictures." My voice was hard.

She sighed heavily. "I can't."

"Wrong answer." I rose. "I will see you in court, then." I headed to the door and tossed over my shoulder. "Oh, and did I mention that Hing said he'd be willing to give you a smaller role in the zombie movie? You'd die early on, but it's a juicy role."

Her eyes flared. "What the hell are you talking about?"

I laughed. "Yeah, apparently, Hing's willing to make a deal with you if you give me those pictures. *Now.*"

She went stiff, her hands clutching her robe like talons.

"That's the thing about Hollywood: everyone has their price, and apparently Hing has his. I have the power to destroy you, yet I'm choosing to help you."

She paced around me. "What do you have over Hing? Did you get the male lead for Sebastian?"

As if I'd ever want him working with her?

I refused to answer that, giving her a shrug.

She started crying, mumbling about sagging skin and cottage cheese legs.

I ignored her hysterics and helped myself to a glass of water. My body language screamed in-control, but I was pushing myself to deal with her. Even though I'd never prance myself across national television, I wanted her to believe it. Offering her this deal was the only way to get rid of her forever.

"You have ten seconds." I tapped at my watch.

She immediately called Harry, who informed her that he'd just gotten off the phone with Hing, who said that if Blair did what I asked—whatever it was—then the smaller role in the zombie movie was hers. She dried her fake tears, and five minutes later, I left her house with her camera, her phone, her laptop, and an envelope of photos.

Violet was back. Like a boss.

☙

An hour later, I could barely contain my excitement for the coming night. Just a few more hours, and I'd be able to tell Sebastian everything. I'd already explained everything to Mila. She'd spent hours with Sebastian yesterday, working on different press statements in case the pictures went live. She'd spoken with a couple of reporters to test out the waters, but Blair had never come forward. Now she never would.

But today, I needed an outfit, a bring-back-your-mojo kind of dress.

I gazed around at the pricey boutique that definitely had a Frederick's of Hollywood vibe to it with itty-bitty outfits and stiletto shoes.

But I didn't want too sexy. This was a charity event.

I slanted a look at Mila. "I take it we aren't here for your usual?"

"What's my usual?" She came to a stop in front of a black lace teddy.

"Pencil skirts, cardigans in pastel colors, pearls, anything that screams librarian with a hard-on for rock stars."

"Don't make fun of me." She poked me with her pink purse.

"I'm not . . . okay, maybe I am, but you have to admit you have a certain style about you."

"Style?"

"You know, like Hello Kitty vomited up a Mother Theresa version of itself."

She put her French manicured nails on her hips. "Maybe I want some sexy holey jeans and—and a set of garters, and a leather-sequined jumpsuit with a big black rhinestone belt—"

I groaned. "Don't wear all that at one time. Promise me."

"You think you know me, but I *could* get a tattoo or a body piercing if I wasn't so terrified of needles . . ." she trailed off, a sad expression on her face that made me chuckle.

Aw. She was gorgeous the way she was, and I secretly thought Spider got off on it too. I leaned in. "Have you talked to Spider lately?"

She shook her head. "No, and I don't want to talk about him. What's going on with Sebastian? Have you talked to him?"

I exhaled. "No, but I did send him a text that the pictures were in my possession and that I'd explain everything later. He tried to call me, but I'm not ready to talk to him. I'm still working with Hing on some details."

"I love how you love him," Mila said softly. "You're sacrificing your privacy for him."

Yes, I'd sold the journal to Hing. "It was for both of us. I couldn't let Blair destroy his career and my life. There comes a point where you just have to stand up and fight for yourself." I suddenly smiled, for once the memory of my father filling me with joy. "My dad always said that the remedy is in the poison."

Mila smirked. "Hmmm, does that mean I should just screw Spider and get him out of my system?"

I shrugged. "Maybe."

She bit her lip. "Back to Sebastian, he's talking of getting on the road soon. He wants to get out of LA for a while. I think—I think he's hurting." She sent me a sad smile. "I'll still stay here in LA, though."

"But—but he can't do that. I'm staying here—and the orphanage."

"But what about your career, V? If you're not going to New York, then what?"

I got giddy with excitement. "Okay, well, this morning I called the chancellor at the Manhattan School of Music and we talked. I explained how I couldn't leave, and he said he'd put in a good word for me at the LA College of Music. He knows a few of the deans there, and he said they'd love to have me. Later, maybe, once my confidence is built up—I can apply for the symphony here."

Mila smiled. "I'm happy for you. Just don't leave Sebastian hanging if you can't be with him."

Of course I wanted to be with him.

I picked a red silk dress off the rack and held it up to my neck. Silky and with a plunging neckline in the front and back, it was gorgeous and not even practical for playing the violin.

Mila grinned. "You'll need tape to hold it in place. I say it's perfect."

I found my size and headed toward the dressing room.

"Why don't you pick out something for yourself?"

She focused on the lingerie section to her right. "Maybe I will."

ை

That night, I busied myself taking care of last-minute gala details at the Wilshire Hotel. The hotel staff scurried around setting up tables and the bar while the Vital Rejects roadies checked-in to set-up the music. The staff set-up the podium too, where the honored speaker was a California Senator, thanks to my connections in New York.

Everything was on schedule.

Sebastian and Spider swaggered in just as the last table had been covered and dishes put out. All the pieces were in play, and tonight was my last chance to put everything on the line for him. Whether he loved me or not, I was willing to give him every part of me. I'd decided to roll the dice and live one day at a time.

He stalked around the room looking divine in designer jeans and his notorious mink coat from his music video. He looked like a sexy blond gangster, but I knew better. He was deliciously sweet.

I watched him smile and sign autographs.

He was *it*. And I didn't just mean star quality, but I meant *it* for me. I'd do anything for him because even though I'd said that loving means losing, it doesn't. Loving means sacrificing.

His eyes flicked over at me, and I straightened my red dress, then my hair. I took a step toward him.

Some of the crowd parted, leaving us standing in front of each other. He ran his eyes over me, and I quivered at the need blazing in his gaze. He took a step toward me, a determined look on his face. I licked my lips, preparing my words.

But a fan walked up to him. And then Mrs. Smythe walked up to me.

The kids from the orphanage arrived via a bus. I greeted them at the door and Mrs. Smythe then led them to where Sebastian and Spider were on the stage. They showed the kids their instruments and did another round of autographs for them.

I couldn't take it any longer. I made my way up to the stage. His eyes followed me the entire way.

I said hi to the kids, but they really only had eyes for the guys.

He jumped down from the stage. "I hope you don't mind that I worked it out with Mrs. Smythe to let the kids come early. I've done the guitar lessons, but not everyone at the orphanage has gotten to meet us." He smiled uncertainly.

"No, thank you for thinking of it. The kids love it."

He looked down, almost seeming shy. "I see why you help them. It's liberating in how it makes you feel. Like you're making a difference. Doing something important. I want to do more of that kind of thing."

"Sebastian—"

"V—"

We both spoke at the same time and then stopped.

"I'm sorry I pushed you away yesterday," I said softly.

"I'm sorry I let you. Look, can we go somewhere and talk before this gets started? There's something I need to tell you."

Hing chose that moment to enter the room. "I should stay here and greet people."

Sebastian sighed, his eyes following mine. "You're changing, V. I mean I like seeing you grow, and if it means you're leaving me, then I'm okay with it."

"What? No, I'm not leaving you."

Just then Blair walked in and made a beeline for us. Sebastian's mouth opened as she dropped a sizable check in my hand and gave us each cheek pecks. "Thank you darling, for everything. I adore you both to the moon and back. Here's my fifty thousand along with an additional ten." She smiled brightly and waltzed off in a haze of perfume.

Sebastian had gone pale. "What the fuck? Am I in Bizarro World?" He grabbed my hand and started walking for the exit doors that led out into the hotel. "I don't know what just happened, but I'm taking you out of here."

"I told you I had her taken care of," I said.

"How?"

I came to a halt. "Stop. I can't do another walk-in cooler episode with you. I have guests."

He ignored me and pulled me out into the hall. "I don't see any coolers. How about that room to the left?" He didn't wait for my answer but walked across the hall and pulled me inside.

I looked around at the mop and broom. "The cleaning closet? Really?"

"Doesn't matter where we are, I'll always want you." He tilted my face up. "I hate fighting with you, V. I've been miserable for the past twenty-four hours, and it has little to do with my career, but all to do with you."

"I know." I touched his face. He looked different. Softer. As if he couldn't take not touching me too, his thumb rubbed my bottom lip.

"Did you know that I could stare at you for hours? You're like a fucking Picasso painting. And your eyes . . . don't even get me started. I want to wake up to them every day for the rest of my life."

Then he kissed me. I moaned as he pressed me up against the wall, his hips fitting against me.

He pulled back, his gaze tender. "I have a confession to make, so bear with me. First off, when it comes to Geoff, I kinda go bonkers. Because I know that if he loved you once with just an iota of the way I love you, then he's never going to be over you completely. I know I need to work on my trust issues. I know I have a messed-up way of looking at girls, but here's the thing I figured out . . . you are *not* those girls. You never will be. I've known you were different from the first moment I watched you play, and if you want to go to New York, then I'll suck it up. Hell, I'll go to couples therapy to make sure I don't let it blow up in our faces. I'll move to Manhattan. I never should have walked off from you yesterday. I was upset thinking you would leave me, and it colored everything I said."

"You love me?" I clutched his arms.

He pressed his forehead against mine. "I do. You're part of me. You're in my heart, in my brain. I've touched you, made love to you, tasted you. I can't ever forget that, and knowing you and your beauty on the inside, I'm never going to be able to watch stars or comets without thinking of you. I'm never going to be able to eat a cheese puff or watch *Star Wars* without wishing you were beside me."

His hand drifted up to touch my hair. "I fell for you so hard it scared me, and I couldn't admit it to myself. I was scared of being used. Scared of losing the most important thing in my life."

Elation soared. *He loved me.*

He continued. "Before I got your message about the pictures, I threatened Blair today that I'd go public about our fake relationship. I told her I was in love with you and that I wanted to marry you and surely she had a decent bone—"

"Married?" I sucked in a breath.

He nodded. "Someday you'll be Mrs. Sebastian Tate."

"You're so sure?"

He swept his hands around his chest. "Have you taken a good look at this sexy piece of male? Chicks are dying to get with me."

I slapped his arm. "Blair? She listened to you?"

He shrugged. "She told me you had the pics, and then I got crazy worried. What did you give her? Please tell me it wasn't money."

We'd both been busy, protecting the other.

I touched his face, his shoulders, his chest, my hands finding their resting place over his heart. "I—I sold my personal story to Hing so he can develop it into a movie. I got a few million in the process, along with an assurance that Blair will get a tiny part in the current movie he's making."

He paled, a wrinkle between his brows. "Why would you do that to yourself? You hate attention."

"But I can do it one time, especially if we're together, and then once the entire story has been told, no one will care. It will all be laid bare. Raw. Just like my music. I also have complete say on everything, even down to who they cast." Emotion clogged my throat. "I—I chose you."

"What do you mean you chose *me*?"

"Yes, it's my life, but it's going to be told from a guy's point of view." I smiled softly. "Yours."

Instead of looking elated, he looked confused, his eyes searching mine. "I love you so much, but I can't allow this to happen. It's insane for you to open yourself up like that."

I shook my head. "I *want* to tell my story. I didn't at first, but that was before I realized how much life I have to live. I want others to see how my life was and most of all, how I survived the grief. Because I have. And the money will keep the orphanage running for years." I smiled. "My heart aches to see you—playing *me*. Because you have been where I am. You know my pain."

I kissed him, chuckling a little at his still stunned face. "I love you, silly. I'd do anything for you."

He closed his eyes and then opened them, a dawning light of wonder in them. "I love you with or without this movie." He bent his head to me. "You are the most beautiful person I've ever met. Inside and out."

I grinned. "It gets better. I'm not going to New York. The orphanage is where I want to be right now." I toyed with the button on his shirt, feeling shy. "Maybe I could go on the road with you in between my semesters at school."

He picked me up and twirled me around. "That is my dream, V."

He pulled a piece of paper out of his jeans. "I wrote a song for you. I've actually been working on it for weeks, and I know it's too early to sing it in public because I didn't want to put the spotlight on you—but may I?" He held it up.

I felt myself glowing. I nodded.

"With your permission, I'd like to make it the first track on the next album. Spider agrees."

I leaned against the wall. Out of breath.

"I don't have my guitar, but it's so powerful that a cappella suits it. You ready?"

I nodded, and he whipped out of his coat and tossed it on the floor. He hummed to get the right pitch. Then he snapped his fingers to a beat in his head, emotion evident on his face, and sang.

Get up, dress and eat,
Move my fingers, my feet.
Play my popular song,
All day long.

Violin Girl in my dreams,
I got it bad it seems.
Dark and twisted,
Music with skin.

I saw you there,
Across the way.
Play your song,
Laying it bare.

Date girls, drink champagne,
Try to forget the pain.
Weep, sweat, and plead,
Violin Girl, you make me bleed.

Quote Romeo and Juliet like a fool,
When all I wanted was to be cool.
Did you know they end in tragedy?

Violin Girl in my dreams,
I got it bad it seems.
Dark and twisted,
Music with skin.

I saw you there,
Across the way.

Play your song,
Laying it bare.

Sit on a couch, watch a vampire show,
Kiss and make love til we blow.
Fall in love under the sky,
I'll take it all, the comet too,
We'll fly.

Violin Girl in my dreams,
I got it bad it seems.
Dark and twisted,
Music with skin.

I saw you there,
Across the way.
Play your song,
Laying it bare.

I saw you there,
I saw you there,
I saw you there . . .

Violin Girl,
Will you be mine,
Be mine.
Be mine.

Silence fell when he ended the song.

Sometimes in your life you just know things, and I knew with certainty that he loved me beyond measure.

He took me back in his arms and wiped my tears. "That song is the first song to the rest of my life."

I bit my lip.

"V, don't cry. It was supposed to make you happy."

"I love you so much." I melted against him. "Kiss me."

He kissed me for a long time.

"We should go," I whispered against his mouth a bit later.

"First, I want you to come, V. Right here before we go out there and blow them away with our music." He slid his hands inside my panties, his fingers working me, sending tingles over my body. I shivered at the need coursing through me.

"I will never get enough of you," he growled.

"What about you?" I gasped out.

"Ride my fingers, V, and when this night is over, you're mine in about a million different ways."

I nodded. Whatever he wanted. Him. *Us.*

I tossed my head back against the wall while his lips and fingers took me to the brink faster than I'd ever been. I clutched his shoulders and held on while he ravaged my skin, my lips, my soul. My body ached to relieve the need I read in his own eyes, and I tried to touch him, but he wouldn't let me. "Just you, V. Just you. Always."

Heat gathered in my spine.

I cried out his name when I combusted, and he groaned with me.

We collapsed against each other and I wasn't sure who was holding up whom.

He smoothed back my hair. "V? I want to tell the world that you're mine. I want to shout it out. Is that crazy?"

I smiled softly. "No."

"You make me a better man. I promise you, right here, I

will love you until the day I die. I will do everything in my power to make sure you're happy. Forget Hollywood, forget music. If there's no you, I'm lost anyway."

"We're going to have it all and more. I'm due."

"Due?"

I pressed a gentle kiss to his lips, feeling the last vestiges of my doubt fade away. "Fairy dust."

CHAPTER 24

"Just so you know, I'm not a fairy, but fairy dust is pretty cool."
—Sebastian Tate

WE STRAIGHTENED OUR CLOTHES AND WENT BACK TO THE banquet. After the speaker and meal were over, we took the stage like we'd practiced the week before. She sat on a stool between us. Protected. As it should be.

I took the microphone, gazed out over the crowd, and poured on the charm that came easily to me.

"I've been told that so far we've raised half a million dollars tonight in donations. How's that for a successful party?"

Lots of clapping ensued with a few catcalls. A few guests took up chanting—mostly the kids who sat the closest to the stage. I grinned and Spider took a big bow, rolling his hands out to the crowd as he strutted around in his blue mink like a peacock.

I raised my hand and spoke over the applause. "You may not know this, but LA is my hometown. From my heart, thank you for coming out and supporting this great cause. It's an honor to be here tonight on this stage with the sponsor of the event, Miss Violet St. Lyons." I cleared my throat. "We have a very special treat for you. V has agreed to play a song with us tonight."

I took off my mink, tossed it on a stool, and turned back to a cheering crowd.

Spider started in with his bass guitar, the sound deep and

melodic. Rich with a twist of grunge. The notes rang clear and slow as V kicked in a few bars later, cutting into me like a knife, the prick of pain in the music personifying *her*.

Elation lit me as I turned to watch her play. There she was, just a simple girl on stage cradling a violin, her music enough to make the hairs on your arms stand up.

She wasn't leaving. She believed in us. She loved me. I loved her.

We played the song and the audience went nuts. Sometimes in your life you just know things, and my gut knew with certainty that that song would blow up the charts and that tonight wouldn't be the last time V performed with us on stage.

The song ended, and I took a deep bow, grabbed V's hand and dashed off stage.

It wasn't the end of our set, but I had to kiss her. I fused our lips together and everything else faded away.

It was the beginning of a thousand stage exits we'd take together.

EPILOGUE

Reunion

AT THE BRIARWOOD ACADEMY FIVE YEAR REUNION, A ROCK STAR, an heiress, a former Hello Kitty lookalike who did *not* wear pink, an Englishman, a prima donna ballerina, a pre-med student, a sexy genius, a gym owner, and a slew of high society people converged in the gymnasium of the prep school in Highland Park, Texas. It was a virtual kaleidoscope of the rich and famous. Limousines, high-octane sports cars and foreign imports dotted the parking lot. More champagne was consumed that night than at any other reunion, guests would later claim.

It was the party of the year—according to Emma East, the organizer and local resident who'd never gone to New York and become an actress, but had instead found herself stuck in her hometown, twenty pounds heavier and married to Matt Dawson, the father of her four children.

When Sebastian Tate strolled in the place with a gorgeous violinist on his arm, she peed herself. Literally. She'd never ex-pected him to be the one who made it big and she berated her-self for not being true to him. Her husband had recently given her the clap, and when he showed up to the party with the sec-retary he was banging, they got into a girl-fight with lots of hair pulling and cheek slapping. Emma left the party early with a ripped dress and a pee stain on the back.

When Sebastian saw Emma for the first time in five years,

all he felt was a big fat nothing, except regret that he'd wasted a lot of time and energy thinking about her. In truth, she'd done him a favor. If things had been different and he'd ended up with Emma, he likely would have never left Texas. Her betrayal proved that sometimes bad things can turn into the best things in our lives.

Sebastian and Violet danced most of the night, in between laughing with their friends. Magazines and tabloids everywhere had announced that she'd just signed a movie deal for ten million dollars and he'd agreed to star in it. They'd also come out publicly about their relationship. As far as his love for the spotlight and her tendency to hide, they'd learned to balance each other out. They kept a low profile, and V was collaborating with the Vital Rejects on their next album. One year later that album would win the Vital Rejects two Grammys: Song of the Year for the song Sebastian wrote for Violet and Record of the Year.

They continued their work with the orphanage and would later open another facility where most of the kids came from Sebastian's old neighborhood. You'd often find the couple hanging out by the pool, stargazing, or playing with their dogs.

Blair left the gala that night thinking she was on top of the world. Apparently blackmailing perfectly nice people and being a bitch seemed to work. Later that week, she'd fallen madly in lust with an eighteen-year-old waiter who worked at Java and Me. They got trashed and drove all night to Vegas where they got married in an Elvis Presley wedding chapel. He divorced her three months later. There was no prenup.

One night she went to the movies and watched Sebastian star in Violet's movie, *Very Twisted Things*. It moved her so much that she repented of her sins and joined a cult of women who only wore white, shaved their heads, and hung out in airports.

Wilson ended up marrying his sexy neighbor, Mrs. Milano who wore sparkly gold bikinis everywhere she went. Without grandkids of his own, he'd often dog-sit for Violet and Sebastian.

Harry deeply regretted being a sorry agent to Sebastian. Once *Very Twisted Things* hit the big screen it would earn Sebastian an Academy Award nomination for Best Actor. He wouldn't win that year, but he did get to pick and choose his roles after that. Music and V, however, always came first.

Geoff went back to New York. He'd loved Violet since he was twenty and losing her to some rock-and-roll dude was depressing. He dated Paris Hilton for a while, but no one stirred his heart. One afternoon while at his Hampton beach house, he saw someone caught in the riptide and dashed out to save her. Turned out she was a bassoonist with the New York Symphony who lived in the Upper East Side and wore cardigans everywhere. It was a match made in Manhattan. They married and lived happily ever after.

Dear Reader,

Thank you for reading *Very Twisted Things*. I hope you enjoyed Sebastian and Violet's story as much as I loved writing it. If you want more passion and angst, Declan and Elizabeths book *Dirty English* is available now: just head straight to the Amazon store to get the entire full-length standalone novel. It is currently FREE in Kindle Unlimited!

And don't worry, Spider will get his story told as well because . . .

THE BRITISH ARE COMING! THE BRITISH ARE COMING! THE BRITISH ARE COMING!

Enjoy!
Ilsa Madden-Mills

Sign up below for my newsletter to receive a FREE Briarwood Academy novella ($2.99 value) plus get insider info and exclusive giveaways!
www.ilsamaddenmills.com/contact

ALSO BY
ILSA MADDEN-MILLS

All books are standalone stories with brand new couples and are currently FREE in Kindle Unlimited.

Briarwood Academy Series
Reading Order:
Very Bad Things
Very Wicked Things
Very Twisted Things

Dirty English
Filthy English
Spider

Fake Fiancée

I Dare You
I Bet You

The Last Guy (w/Tia Louise)
The Right Stud (w/Tia Louise)

ABOUT THE AUTHOR

Wall Street Journal, New York Times, and *USA Today* bestselling author Ilsa Madden-Mills writes about strong heroines and sexy alpha males that sometimes you just want to slap. A former high school English teacher and elementary librarian, she adores all things *Pride and Prejudice*; Mr. Darcy is her ultimate hero. She loves unicorns, frothy coffee beverages, vampire books, and any book featuring sword-wielding females.

*Please join her FB readers group, Unicorn Girls, to get the latest scoop as well as talk about books, wine, and Netflix:

www.facebook.com/groups/ilsasunicorngirls

You can also find Ilsa at these places:

Website:
www.ilsamaddenmills.com

News Letter:
www.ilsamaddenmills.com/contact

Book + Main:
bookandmainbites.com/ilsamaddenmills

Made in the USA
Coppell, TX
17 November 2022

86560070R00136